PORTIA OAKESHOTT, DINOSAUR VETERINARIAN

PORTIA OAKESHOTT, DINOSAUR VETERINARIAN

FIVE SCIENCE FICTION SHORT STORIES

RAYMUND EICH

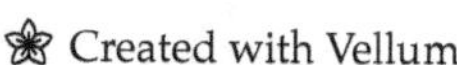 Created with Vellum

CONTENTS

RIDDLEPIGS AND THE CRYLA

RIDDLEPIGS AND THE CRYLA

The quadrotor flier banked over fields and paddocks aligned with the contours of the land. From just above the northern horizon, the K6 sun, Stella Australis A, threw shadows of houses, barns, and scattered groves of oaks and elms long distances over the slender ribbons of purple-black living asphalt and slate gray gravel linking the human habitations to the nearest town.

All familiar sights. Portia Oakeshott's gaze went due south. Pasture land gave way to the perimeter strip of untamed grasses dotted with trees. Judging from the color and texture of foliage, some were elms and oaks, but the trees common to the inhabited territories of New New South Wales shared the terrain with deeper, wilder greenery: cycads, conifers, woody ferns. Further south, between the perimeter and the jagged, snow-capped peaks of the Lesser South Polar Range peeking through the blue haze at the horizon, the deeper green thickened. The dinosaur preserve.

She'd entered the preserve on training missions, but now was the first time no senior veterinarian mentored her.

The quaddy descended toward the last farmstead. Four hundred meters away, cycads spread palm-like fans of leaves high over the ground. The barbed-wire fence of the last paddock ran between squared-off poles striped indigo and scarlet. Perimeter markers. Below, a rambling house and a steel-walled barn. Though the quaddy descended with the house and barn between them, a herd of pigs squealed and fled to the corner of their enclosure farthest from the buzzing machine.

"The riddlepigs are still spooked from the cryla," said McAdams, the ecologist. His booming voice easily overpowered the rotors' whine. From under wavy, graying hair, his bulging eyes watched the pigs stampede to a different corner of their pen.

Portia shivered. The pigs had good reason to be spooked. The farm's surveillance video left no room for doubt. The forehead crest running laterally just behind the eyes, the two three-toed legs jumping over barbed wire, the rows of small sharp teeth clamping on the back of a pig's neck. *Cryolophosaurus.* A female—the forehead crest was smaller and a duller mix of orange and red than a male's. Still young, barely two meters tall and only six meters from snout to tail-tip.

Only. A theropod, the closest thing to a *T. rex* near Earth's south pole during the Jurassic. The apex predator of the dinosaur preserve.

She'd played the video enough times on the thirty-minute flight from Margarettown to memorize the sights and sounds. Sirens roared out the same notes as the repulsion markers. Pigs squealed. Dogs bared their teeth and the hair on their backs bristled as they barked at the green intruder. A man's voice, shouting curses. The deafening bangs of rifle fire.

Three shots, then the cryla fled, jumping as high and running even faster than a king kangaroo. Did it favor its left leg? Was that a red crease on the thigh?

They touched down on a grassy area thirty meters from the house. The rotors whined to a stop. They climbed out of the cabin into warm summer air. Portia yanked her medical kit from under her seat. They ducked under the rotor struts. Gravel crunched under their boots on their way to the house's front door.

Centered on a dark green lawn of gene-engineered grass, the house showed native stone walls, wide windows facing north, a metal roof with a shallow pitch and rippled and painted brick-red in imitation of spanish tile. Two saplings, protected by cylindrical cages, grew on the sides of a flagstone path. The shine of Stella A tinged the house a warm orange. A cozy place for a quiet life, if that's what you wanted.

The front door opened. A woman came onto the front step and shut the door on a quartet of barking dogs. The light emphasized fine lines and spots of middle age. Brown hair straggled loose from a headband tucked behind large and saggy ears. She raised her hand to shield her hazel eyes against the low sun. Her gaze jittered to the Blighland Dinosaur Preserve corporation's logo on Portia and McAdams' shirts. Her eyes settled on his shirt, following the ring of dinosaurs encircling the outline of the continent. "G'day," she said with a guarded, nasal voice.

McAdams stepped forward. "G'day, ma'am. You're—" He obviously double-checked the name through his neuronal interface. "—Ms. O'Connor?"

"Gwendolyn."

"The dino company sent us from Margarettown. My name's McAdams and the young lady is Dr. Oakeshott."

"Doctor.... A veterinarian?" Gwendolyn O'Connor cradled her cheek with her palm. "Of course a vet. I'm still not thinking straight after the cryla attack." Her eyes sharpened their focus. "Never mind me. My husband. He's in the barn with her. She's still alive."

Portia's heart quickened. A chance to treat an injured dinosaur! Creatures reconstructed from fossilized bone, genetic extrapolation from modern birds, imagination, and Aussie pride. A dream born fifteen standard years earlier, with toys on the floor of her bedroom thousands of klicks away. A dream that survived teen angst and a challenging courseload at university.

A dream coming to fruition mere moments from now. Her voice trembled. "Which way?"

The woman gestured at an extension of the gravel lane that rounded the house.

"We'll take a look straight away," said McAdams. Portia stepped down to the lawn before he finished speaking.

"Come by the house when you're done," Gwendolyn O'Connor said. "I'll put on the billy for a spot of tea."

"I'd love a cuppa," Portia said over her shoulder, "but duty calls."

Her feet reached the gravel lane. She strode even faster.

A barn clad in steel, freshly painted and undented, twice the size of the house. Solar panels covered a roof pitched steeply to face north. The gravel lane ended at a rolling door with a ramped concrete slab sticking out from under. A strip of bare dirt led from the end of the gravel to a walk-through door with a dog flap.

McAdams caught up with her as she opened the door and led the way inside.

Her boots scraped to a halt on the concrete floor. Smells battered her nose. Pigs and their manure; grain pellets in a hopper; blood.

A man sitting on his shins looked up. A broad-brimmed hat pushed back on his head revealed a receding hairline and a jutting chin. His hand absently petted the flank of a sow. The female pig lay on its side, breathing quickly and shallowly, a plaintive whimper in its throat. The blood came from three slashes running from a now-mangled teat across its belly to its ribcage.

Portia frowned. She peered around the barn. "Where's the cryla?"

"The cryla?" The man had a thick accent. "Who'n the bloody hell cares about the cryla?"

His mild obscenity didn't register. Feet frozen, Portia's gaze darted around the room. She inhaled through her open mouth. The overpowering smell. No cryla. A pig. Blood.

Her hands jittered at her sides. No cryla—

"Dr. Oakeshott." McAdams' voice, respectful yet authoritative. "Take a look at the man's pig."

Her cheeks burned. The pig—you're a vet—

She stepped forward. A lesson from one of her professors about how to practice came to mind. Fake it till you make it. "Allow me, Mr. O'Connor." She crouched on the concrete, next to the puddle of thickening blood, and set down the medical kit.

O'Connor rose on stiff knees and shuffled backwards. His jutting chin was a like a transmission antenna, radiating distrust of her abilities.

One steadying breath. She'd trained on animals ranging from house cats to thoroughbred horses. Including pigs.

"There there," she said gently to the sow. She checked the wounds from the cryla's front claws. Still seeping blood, and that one teat would never again suckle a piglet, but no damage to internal organs. Including whichever human organ it grew as a clone for transplant to some rich person in a distant city. She'd always assumed they were called riddlepigs for being like a jigsaw puzzle, until a boy at university had bored her on their first and only date by telling her they were named for their inventor long ago on Earth.

She reached into her kit for two vials, a coagulant and an antibacterial. Stop the bleeding and prevent infection. She snapped open the coagulant and squirted the contents into the slashes. The pig squirmed when the gel touched its wounds. Its feet kicked for the concrete but it couldn't get up.

Next, restore blood volume. From her medkit she drew a vacuum-sealed pack of red powder and a water distiller that looked like a backpacker's portable kettle. She snapped the pack into place and rested her fingers on the threaded cap of the distiller's inlet reservoir. "I need a liter of water," she said as she turned her head. "The cleaner the better, but it needn't be sterile."

Her cheeks burned again. The two men talked about her.

"It's her second day in country," McAdams said. "Literally. We were going to ease her in with routine survey work when you called with this emergency—"

"Water, please," Portia said more forcefully. "We're taking a look at Mr. O'Connor's pig, aren't we?"

Did McAdams smile or smirk? His voice proved it a smirk. "Yes, doctor."

O'Connor nodded and went to a spigot. For a three-count, water drummed into a plastic bucket.

The farmer carried over the bucket while Portia opened the cap and pulled a funnel from her kit. He poured. Some water splashed out of the bucket to the floor, but most entered the funnel. The distiller's flex-walled reservoir bulged.

A green light came on and the distiller dinged. "That's enough, thanks."

The farmer backed away. Portia pressed a button. Purified water filled the pack of red powder, rehydrating a cross-linked, isotonic solution of a hemoprotein. After it finished, she squeezed her hand around the sow's leg to help veins stand up. She flipped a flexible smart needle away from the hemoprotein pack, touched it to the sow's leg, and the needle did the rest.

The sow kicked feebly as the needle entered. "There there," she said. A tiny motor whined as it pumped hemoprotein solution into the pig's bloodstream.

The sow relaxed. Portia did too.

After the bag emptied, she sprayed white foam bandage over the slash marks and a hand's width of margin all around. While it set, she rose and said to O'Connor, "She's out of danger. Have your local vet come out tomorrow to check on her."

"I'll do that." O'Connor studied the hissing foam, then scowled at McAdams and Portia. "And I'll send the bill for all the damage your pet done to your home office, rely on it."

McAdams raised a hand before Portia could speak. "The company always pay promptly, and fair value, for something like this."

"Bloody cryla snapped her jaws on Kidneys. Ripped two vertebrae out the back of his gelded neck. Most needed transplant organs, kidneys are. And don't tell me the customer can go on dialysis while we raise a piglet with new cloned kidneys. Inconvenient as hell for her and it makes me look like a right galah."

Portia frowned at his indelicate language. "Mr. O'Connor, there's no—"

"—Need to worry about the cryla," said McAdams to the farmer. "We're going across the perimeter after her."

"That's another thing." O'Connor said, his face redder than before. "The markers. Sirens, the striped colors, all supposed to keep your pets on their side. It didn't work."

"We'll investigate that too. We want to prevent these kind of events as much as you do."

"A bonzer high fence along the back. Three meters, with razor wire on top, pointed out. I'll send a bill for that to your home office, too."

"That's up to you," McAdams said. "We'll show ourselves out."

He led the way back to the quaddy. Portia followed mutely. They climbed in and McAdams spun up the rotors. He flew in a loop, giving the uneasy pigs wide berth. Under an overhang of the barn, a parked tractor held high its front-end loader. In the loader slumped a heap of pink, marred by a spot of reddish-brown.

They flew over a paddock toward the back fence and the line of perimeter markers. The strands of barbed wire ran for many klicks in either direction. Portia couldn't tell where O'Connor's strech of fence ended and the neighbors' began, let alone make out where the cryla had crossed. But McAdams guided the quaddy with a purposeful look in his eyes, over the fence, over a four-meter-tall perimeter marker and an even taller cycad. Fronds writhed in the quaddy's downdraft as he descended to a patch of open ground colonized by yellow-green grazing grass.

They climbed out. Apply insect repellent with a hiss of the canister. Call the field office with an update relayed through the quaddy's transmitter. Portia pulled out her medical kit and hooked a canteen to a matching patch of loop fabric on the thigh of her cargo pants. Binoculars went on a strap around her neck.

McAdams hefted his backpack. He settled his hat on his wavy hair and snapped the right side of the brim onto the crown. A bin in the cargo compartment popped its lid for him. Out he pulled a rifle, its wide barrel like a black water pipe, and slung it over his shoulder.

Portia let out a breath. The dinosaurs in the preserve weren't the plastic dolls she'd played with as a child. They were wild animals. And something had driven the cryla across the perimeter.

A long and skinny cylinder in the bin caught her attention. "The trank gun." After an uncertain moment, she reached for it. Cool metal in her hands. A tool to heal, not harm.

"Yeah, we might need that," said McAdams. He took the trank gun from her and slung it over his shoulder. A box of tranquilizer darts went into a baggy pocket..

After they loaded, McAdams squinted against the low orange sun as he faced north, toward the nearest perimeter marker, about twenty meters away. "It's reporting proper working order to my neuronal interface. Yours?"

Five seconds to think her way to the data feed coming in from the marker. With smirking judgment in McAdams' bulging eyes, it felt much longer. Finally, her neuronal interface augmented her view of the perimeter marker with signals induced on her optic nerves. Green lights, checkmarks, numbers within ranges. "Mine too." She turned her head up and down the line of perimeter markers as far as intervening trees allowed. The markers' stripes strained her eyes with each little motion of her head. "All clear for a long way, both directions."

McAdams spoke aloud, though his thoughts alone would get picked up by his neuronal interface's dictation software. "'The markers appear functional for at least two hundred meters on either side of where the cryla crossed the perimeter. Dr. Oakeshott agrees.'" The last words struck her as an afterthought.

She ran her gaze over the barbed wire fence. "How can you be so certain she crossed here?"

"I watched the whole video. Didn't you?"

"Of course I did. But—" She gestured at cycads and elms, perimeter markers and barbed wire strung taut along narrow metal posts. "It all looks the same."

"Keep your eyes open and you'll learn some bushcraft." McAdams took a few steps through shin-high grass toward an imaginary line running from the distant barn to the tall cycad. He stopped and pointed at a grass tuft. "Like that."

Was he making fun of her? "Like what?" Then she saw a cluster of bent stalks. "Oh."

"Come on. What else do you see?"

She looked around. Three meters farther from the perimeter, a shape like a V with a dot under the point marred a patch of soft yet barren soil. From the shape and the size—longer than McAdams' foot—

"The cryla went—" Portia extended her arm in the direction opposite the V's point. Away from the farm. Deeper into the transition zone. Toward the preserve beyond the line of markers hidden by reconstructed Mesozoic forest.

McAdams adjusted his backpack. The rifle and the trank gun clanked together. He nodded toward the cryla's trail. "Off we go."

Mosquitos buzzed around Portia. The ground, damp from spring rains, clung to the soles of her boots. They didn't carry flashlights, but they wouldn't need them. At 80° south latitude and close to the summer solstice, the sun, though low in the sky, would never set.

They trudged on. The grasses thinned out. In their place grew mosses, dwarf ferns, and fuzzy yellow fungi. Despite the change in ground cover, now that she knew what to look for, the theropod blazed a trail no one could miss. Tracking her became so easy that Portia's mind refocused on what McAdams had said in the barn. "I might be new, but I don't appreciate being made light of because of it."

McAdams paused. He slapped at a mosquito on the side of his neck. His bulging eyes squinted. "Make light of you? What do you mean?"

"When I tended O'Connor's sow. 'It's only her second day in-country.' I'm new to the bush but I'm not a clueless city girl. I earned my vet cert."

"Yes, you did. *And* it's only your second day in-country."

"What has that to do with anything?"

"You were flustered when we went into the barn. I had to explain that away."

"Perhaps I was," Portia said. "A little. But what does it matter, what thinks some farmer we'll never see again?"

McAdams ripped his canteen loose from its hook-and-loop patch. "Crikey, what do they teach you about community affairs during your training?"

At the company's campus near Port Bounty, a thousand klicks away on the continent's north shore, all the classrooms in the training facility had looked the same. "Do your best to represent the company and the dinos to everyone you meet. That's all I remember."

After a slug of water, McAdams slammed closed the canteen's stopper. "Mangy bastard desk jockeys, your pardon. I'm going to tell what they should've but didn't."

She folded her arms. "Please do."

He fixed his bulging eyes on her. "Half the people of rural Blighland hate us. The other half are primed to."

"Half the people?" Her arms hugged her torso tighter. "Have there been so many attacks by crylos, or others?"

"Got nothing to do with dino attacks on livestock. It goes back fifty standard years, to when the Crown granted the company the land in the first place. If the locals had their druthers, they'd have riddlepig farms from here to the lesser range." He waved a hand that direction.

"It's all about money?"

"Most things are."

"But tourists to the preserve. From Cookland. From off-planet!"

"Tourists bring in money? True. But their money doesn't enter the accounts of riddlepig farmers. Or the med techs who harvest the cloned organs. Or the express pilots who fly from here to Port Bounty or from there to the big cities on Cookland."

"You needn't lecture me."

He rolled his eyes. "You're closer to my eldest daughter's age than mine. Time to keep moving."

Around a scowl, Portia nodded. They set off.

"The locals have powerful allies," McAdams said. "They've returned the same member of parliament for decades now. And they lobby key ministers in HM's government. Agriculture. Health. Rural Affairs. The Crown has a million square klicks in eastern Blighland to grant to someone in the next few standard years. Every incident like this one is another sand grain on the balance against us. Oh what's this?"

He stooped near the cryla's track. A fern tree's fronds striped his face with orange sunlight and shadow. His bulging eyes peered at something on the grass.

Portia came closer. Against the deep green of a moss patch growing on a knee-high boulder, deep red immediately caught her gaze.

"O'Connor hit her at least once." McAdams straightened. "Take a sample for the sequencer."

"Yes, of course." Portia unslung her medical kit. She pulled out a sterile pipette, tore the package open. She drew up half a milliliter of the cryla's blood. A quick press injected the blood sample into the portable DNA sequencer.

"That'll work while we hike," McAdams said. He moved forward before she could reply. She followed. Her gaze roved ahead, looking for more blood drops.

And finding them.

Small drops, though. A scratch on a creature as big as the cryla.

Yellow lights blinked back and forth across the palm-sized device, till all the lights flashed green at once. "Sequencing complete," she said.

"Good," said McAdams, without turning.

Portia trudged along after him. A gruff man, though maybe everyone became gruff by their forties. Maybe he had good reason. Half of all rural Blighlanders hated the company? Politicians played footy with everyone's livelihood? The home office didn't train people in things they needed to know?

She cast downturned eyes to the cryla's trail. No grass at all, this deep into the transition zone, but the theropod's distinctive footprint gouged wet soil and scraped moss off rocks. More drops of blood marked the trail, past the second line of perimeter markers, and for two hundred meters further into the preserve proper.

Why did people have to fight one another? She just wanted to help the dinosaurs of the preserve. Did McAdams? Yes, he must. Why else work at this job for decades?

So he wanted to help the dinosaurs, but why didn't everyone else?

A rustle came from behind a dwarf cycad ten meters off the trail. A glimpse of blue-black feathers revealed a flightless grackelsaur, no larger than a raven, engineered purely for this particular niche. Its long beak darted, picking long beetles off the cycad's rippled trunk. The grackelsaur paused in its eating. Its head jittered as it regarded Portia and McAdams, then turned back to eating beetles as the humans walked away.

Maybe people needed to come out here. To see creatures like the grackelsaur. Or to hear—

A deep bellowing came from some distance deeper in the preserve. She looked that way but only saw prehistoric forest of tall ferns and cycads. "Is that a winner?"

"No, that was a tino's call. Don't worry your head about it. I couldn't tell them apart my first day in the bush either." *Wintonotitan* and *Diamantina*, the preserve's two titanosaurs, reconstructed based on Australian fossils.

The *Diamantina* bull bellowed again. "Is he trying to scare off the cryla?"

McAdams raised his hand to ask for silence, then angled his head. The tino bellowed twice more.

The field ecologist's voice boomed in the ensuing quiet. "Not the cryla. He scented a bachelor male lurking around his harem. That was a challenge or a warning."

Portia's shoulders hunched. It wasn't just people who battled one another. A line from an ecology lecture, grandmotherly Dr. Bultas with wise wrinkles around her eyes: *The fiercest struggle is between two creatures fighting for one niche.*

McAdams' gaze tracked along the ground. His eyes stopped and grew even larger than usual. "Our cryla's got bigger problems." He pointed.

Not a drop of blood, but a spill, enough to drip off the cap of a lanky, lime-green mushroom and join a seeping puddle. Granted, and as she'd learned watching clumsy lab partners, ten milliliters could cover a large area.

But the absolute volume wasn't the problem. It was the relative.

She glanced ahead. Blood showed like a painting robot's malfunction. "Why'd she suddenly start bleeding more?"

"Bullet might've worked deeper into her thigh. Bone fragment might've nicked an artery."

How could he sound so cold? "We've got to find her."

"Too right."

Onward. A breeze from the south rustled foliage and chilled their faces. The cryla's track crashed through undergrowth between narrowly-spaced trees. The spacing of footprints showed she limped badly. One left footstep had slipped thirty, forty centimeters when she'd stepped on a flat, wet rock. Blood trickled down a fern's woody trunk.

An individual from a different species of small bird-like creature, dun-colored and winged, with glide membranes attached to its legs, sniffed at blood drops on the ground. Another pure invention, a geyersaur, eater of carrion. The geyersaur looked at them, then patiently hopped away from their approach.

The trees thinned out ahead. In the brighter light, she saw a heap of scat before the breeze carried its smell to her.

McAdams paused and eyed the pile of feces. "Still steaming."

Evenings at a tea shop near her apartment in Port Bounty, she'd drilled on knowledge like identifying dinos from their scat while ignoring young men trying to flirt. "It's got to be hers, but it looks runny—"

Another sniff. A chill shivered down her back. More than the usual distasteful stink of scat. A smell from her dog-and-cat training. An elderly hound, toothless and cancerous, brought in to be euthanized. Whether through age-related incontinence or a sixth sense, the old dog had soiled the floor of the exam room with soft feces stinking of fear.

"We've got to hurry." Portia started forward. McAdams took loping strides to get back in the lead.

They came to the clearing. Amid skeletal trunks and branches left behind by a forest fire, a riot of bright colors smothered the ground. Flowers that looked modern—she could only identify the bright yellow of dandelions—mingled with primitive ones budded from creeping vines. Deep green moss choked the blackened trunks of dead trees. Algae turned puddles into patches of phosphorescent green. Life, cramming as much growth and reproduction into New New South Wales' ten-day spring as it could.

Portia looked for a place to step into the open. McAdams held his arm across her path. "Wait."

"Why?" The wind had picked up and grown colder on her face.

McAdams pointed into the teeth of the wind. Almost directly across the clearing, under the rustling fronds of a barrel-chested cycad, lay the cryla.

Portia looked through her binoculars. The cryla's right side pressed against the cycad's trunk. Though dull, the red and orange of her forehead crest contrasted with textured brown. She curled to the left, trying to protect the wound. Her head feebly stirred toward her left thigh. Her tongue flicked once past her teeth, like a dog or cat licking a wound, but the pink tip came nowhere near the wound.

Her head sagged back against the cycad. Her chest heaved with rapid breaths. Her body uncurled enough to show blood oozing in slow pulses from the entry wound.

Portia's mouth curled downward. Pressure welled behind her eyes. How could a bullet hole so small bring down so large a creature?

"It's clear what we have to do," McAdams said.

Portia nodded. Same as the wounded pig. Stop the bleeding. Restore blood volume. Dress the wound to reduce the risk of infection.

To her side, metal clanked and leather creaked. Good idea. Tranquilize the cryla, else she might snap at the people come to save her. Her gaze still on the wounded theropod, Portia said, "A lower dose than usual. She's in shock...."

McAdams racked the slide on the rifle and raised the stock to his shoulder. Blue plugs joined by a white string filled his ears. "You needn't look at this, Dr. Oakeshott."

"There's no need to euthanize her. Do you hear me? We can save her."

The field ecologist lowered the rifle. He held it by the barrel like a walking stick. "*Can*? Yeah, I reckon. But the moment she hopped the fence onto O'Connor's farm, she signed her death warrant."

"She might wander back across, you're saying?"

"A cryla's never going to run *from* something. The motivation came out of her brain."

"That's no reason to kill her. We, we." Portia groped aimlessly at the air. "We could move her."

"I don't pump that much iron. Do you?"

"Our quaddy...." Not enough lift for tons of theropod. "The company's mega quaddies...." A thousand klicks away, at the staging ground near Port Bounty. Used for delivering eggs and hatchlings to the preserve at the start of each season.

Her gut sank. The home office deployed mega quaddies to establish new species and new ranges. Even if they could get a mega here in time, they wouldn't send one to save one individual.

Portia's lips trembled. *Keep yourself together.* The cryla had to be put down, for the same reason as a family dog that gave in to a fleeting aggressive impulse and bit a child.

But fifteen years aspiring to heal dinosaurs—

All dinosaurs. Not just this one.

She inhaled a sniffling breath. The pressure behind her eyes eased. She fixed her gaze on the wounded cryla. "We do what we must."

McAdams studied her face for a moment, then nodded with approval. "Cover your ears."

She flattened her hands on the sides of her head. He raised the rifle to his shoulder.

The cryla lifted her head, exposing the underside of her jaw. As if she knew, and sought out her fate.

McAdams fired a single shot. Small flying dinosaurs erupted from the edges of the clearing.

The large-caliber round hit the cryla under the jaw and carried into the braincase. She slumped instantly. More merciful than the cocktail of poisons used to euthanize pets.

He lowered the rifle. Portia, her hands. Her ears rang.

Portia rocked on her feet for a second. She hugged her torso. The wind must have picked up. Her voice sounded muffled in her own ears. "I have to examine her post-mortem."

Across the clearing, its wings spread to catch the cold wind from the south, a geiersaur glided to the color-strewn ground a few meters from the cryla's corpse.

WINNER AND THE POACHER

CHAPTER 1

The self-driving rideshare sedan turned off the coast road. On whispers of the electric motor and smooth living asphalt, the sedan carried its passenger between marble colonnades to the neighborhood's entry gate. The bar was down and the sedan obediently stopped and opened its window. Mild latewinter air drifted in, tanged with salt, and bearing the rustle of waves on rocks.

A speaker in the gate kiosk spoke in a firm male voice. "Your name, and who to see."

"Portia Oakeshott. The police called me to 17 Aldersley Lane." The gate bar failed to lift. "I'm with the dino company."

The bar lifted then. The sedan rolled forward, down dark and winding streets nearly empty though it was about 1300 of the local clock. On either side, bathed in the orange-red glow of sunlamps, rambling houses sprawled across vast lots, set back behind towering oaks and wide front lawns, grass cropped as low as a golf fairway's or a footy oval's. The houses invariably faced tall windows to the northern horizon, craving Stella Australis A, last seen two weeks before.

Thank God the sun would rise in just a couple of days.

But not today.

The sedan came to a T-junction, beyond which, and through a grove of eucalyptus in someone's side yard, a faint glimmer of twilight showed the seam between sky and ocean. A right turn, then a stop, three houses ahead. Long but not low. A shed roof sloped north, away from the street.

With a thought through her neuronal interface, Portia transferred two cryptoquid and climbed out. The crash of waves overwhelmed the sound of motor and street as the sedan drove off for its next passenger.

She studied the southern face of the house. Windowless. Doorless? No, follow the flagstones to that gap in the curtain wall, near the west side. The soles of her flats snapped on the pavers. Electric torches flanking the gap pivoted and flooded her with light.

She stopped squinting just as a uniformed policeman emerged from the gap. A round face, jug ears. He gave her an appraising glance up and down. "Sorry, miss. Police business. Please move along."

Portia stopped and crossed her arms. "I'm with the dino company."

The policeman started. He glanced to the side, the common gesture of someone looking up information. "You're Dr. Oakeshott? I was expecting, y'know, some old bloke with the brim snapped up on his digger hat."

"You have me."

The policeman swallowed. "Inspector Leichhardt is expecting you. He's in the lower basement. Go in, turn right, service corridor, fourth door on your right."

Portia went three steps past the policeman and in.

Double doors opened into a gigantic living room, extending the full depth of the house to picture windows facing the twilit ocean. An open sliding glass door let in the sounds of surf and muttering policemen standing on a balcony. The ceiling was vaulted to the sloped roof and striped with skylights. The furniture, all straight lines with a color palette mixing grayscale and natural wood, had the 99% perfect look of bespoke handcrafting.

A rich man's house, if the drive in hadn't tipped her.

She followed the policeman's instructions to the stairwell down. A din of echoes off walls excavated from rock and concrete stairs. At the first landing, she glimpsed a rec room. Picture windows blended with the rock face of the bluff. Billiards, air hockey, robotic craps and black-jack tables. Half-empty liquor glasses and spent vape canisters barnacled each tabletop, like Mesozoic fungi and mosses growing in the dinosaur preserve a thousand klicks to the south.

A rich man's party, interrupted. That might explain the police.

But why a dinosaur veterinarian?

The stairwell ended another five meters down. Bulbs flashed on the other side of a half-open door. Portia sniffed but smelled neither alcohol nor blood. She approached with hesitant steps, and rapped her knuckles on the door.

"Dr. Oakeshott?" A man's voice, smooth and slow. "Come in."

She went into the room. For a moment, her heart seemed to stop.

A space as large as the living room or the rec room, but windowless. And stuffed with mounted dinosaurs. In the middle, dioramas of small and bird-like creatures. A geiersaur's hooked beak ripping flesh from the belly of a minmi flipped on its back like a giant turtle. A grackelsaur snapping a millipede into the air and just touching its jaws to it, prior to swallowing it whole.

Along the walls, mounted heads. There, another minmi, its stolid face surrounded with bony protrusions like an elizabeth collar. There, a strallo, a male *Australovenator*, the bumps on his nasal ridge as bright red-orange as a spring sunset after a volcanic eruption.

Mounted dinosaurs. About two dozen of them.

Yes, the company granted hunting permits, both to thin the numbers of species pushing the preserve's carrying capacity and to bring in revenue from tourists, especially off-worlders. And the taxidermists had respected the trophies enough to pose them true to life, and not dress them in schoolboy uniforms to play cricket. Still, these creatures deserved better. Especially—

Her breath caught. On the far wall, a head so huge it seemed impossible to belong to a once-living creature—

"I don't know those huge plant-eaters well enough," said the man. "Is that a winner or a tina?"

Wintonotitan *can be distinguished from the preserve's other titanosaur,* ***Diamantinasaurus****, by its broader face and more gracile bone structure.*

Wintonotitan's skin is a darker green and may have brownish patches, most commonly on the legs and....

Rehearsing the field guidebook lifted her above flooding emotions for a moment, until she gave the mounted head a closer look. The soft jaw. A mottled spot like a fallen leaf on the sloping brow above the eyes. Her stomach clenched. "A winner cow."

A light strobed somewhere. Portia squeezed shut her eyes.

"Y'know," the man said, "we should let the forensic techs finish taking photos and so on while we talk more."

She opened her eyes enough to see him gesture at the door.

"After you, Dr. Oakeshott." He plainly sensed her unease but didn't want to call her out on it.

She kept her eyes on the half-open door. Easy to do when your vision is turning gray and spotty in the periphery. The crack of her flat soles on concrete treads brought her back enough that she reached ground level without incident, and entered the first room she found.

Motion-activated lights revealed a kitchen, gleaming with stainless steel and gray-black granite. She pulled out a stool and sat at an island counter, where small but heavy-looking appliances sat next to a black glass induction cooktop covered with used glasses and empty beer bottles.

The man followed her. A sticky sound meant he'd trod through spilled beer. He leaned his elbows on the island and angled his head at a paddle full of holes mounted on extra-large stand mixer. "My missus might know what that's for, but I haven't a clue."

She inhaled deeply, and though the stale odors of last night's party filled her nose, the air was fresh enough for her to fully recover. "I'm sorry, I've assumed you're Inspector Leichhardt, but I didn't ask to be certain."

"Quite all right, Doctor. We threw you in the deep end down there."

"I'm pronouncing it correctly? 'Like-heart.'"

"Bang on. Alan Leichhardt, Port Bounty Police." Brown hair salted with gray, brown eyes radiating fine wrinkles from their outer corners. He pushed off the counter and extended his hand. A crisp white cuff extended out of the sleeve of a mass-market blue suit. She shook a hand patterned with calluses.

Her glance darted around the room. "What happened?"

"You can tell, they were having a blowout, everyone's got a gutful, when we got called about a...." He licked his lips and his eyes studied the grain of the granite while he answered. "Can't go into details, ongoing investigation, y'know."

Her cheeks warmed. Something lurid. "And?"

"We're investigating. Then a straggler with boots so wobbly he didn't run off when police were coming pipes up. 'Don't let them see the second basement.' That's probable cause right there. We go down. Pick the lock. And realize we need an expert."

The company granted hunting rights on the preserve, but only when a species needed its numbers managed. Never had the company allowed hunting of winner cows. That stuffed head in the lower basement... Portia shivered. Then through the balcony door and the mansion's open floor plan came the muttered words of the other policemen and the crash of waves on rocks at the base of the bluff. "Was dinosaur poaching the worst crime committed here last night?"

He leaned his elbows on the counter and regarded her with his wrinkled brown eyes. "As you guessed, it wasn't. See, we've locked horns with this fella for years, on stuff that's not quite as—" Leichhardt's tongue darted between his lips and he glanced down. "Every time his father bails him out and lawyers him up. You from Port Bounty, miss—doctor?"

She shook her head. "Esperance Heights, on Cookland." Trees lined with oaks and sweetgums, and the sun rose every day, even in the weeks of winter.

"You wouldn't know the pull the Martinson family has around here, then," Leichhardt said. "The pattern repeated last night. Young Lachlan Martinson went american on us—"

"American?"

"Y'know, like the costume dramas set centuries ago on Earth." Leichhardt put on a funny accent. "'I decline to answer and I'd like to speak with my attorney.' And he won't turn over audio or video from his neuronal interface, and we can't compel him to." He wrinkled his nose, as if the odor of spilled beer had gotten to him. "Importing all that American nonsense into proper Anglo-Australian criminal procedure. There's a reason the Americans lost their hyperpower status...."

He took a breath and his expression softened. "Brambles in the path, mate," he muttered to himself. "Where was I, Dr. Oakeshott?"

"You've never convicted Lachlan Martinson of any other crime he's committed."

"Bang on. And what happened last night." Leichhardt nodded in the direction of the balcony. "We can't let Martinson, or whichever of his guests did it, walk free. So we realized the dinosaurs might be a way to ring him up, like Capone on tax."

Her brow wrinkled.

"Figure of speech. Get him on something minor. Then we use that as a wedge to ring him up on everything else."

"Dinosaur poaching being the wedge." As if that dead winner cow counted for nothing.

He's not saying that. She counts for something, but less than whatever a person suffered here last night.

"Not to make light of it," Leichhardt said, "but bang on. We know under Dinosaur Hunting Act 2749 that your company only allows hunting on the preserve under permit specifying species and sex, and logs DNA information on animals taken. Should be dead simple to see which ones Martinson's taken without permit."

She knew the gist of the Act, but called up the text through her neuronal interface and skimmed it where it was projected on the fingerprint-smudged stainless steel refrigerator door. "He's got an obvious defense. Claim they wandered off the preserve. It's open season then."

"The preserve's got fencing, right?"

Portia shook her head. "It's got a double line of perimeter markers a hundred meters apart. They have passive measures, shape and color striping, that the dinosaurs have been genetically coded to avoid. They react to motion of dinosaurs off the preserve with sirens, ultrasonics, flashing lights, and stench bombs. And shoot video. And the farmers adjoining the preserve invariably run fencing along the back lines of their properties."

Leichhardt rubbed his fingertips against the base of their thumb. " From all that...."

"Martinson could claim the dinosaurs wandered off the preserve, but he'd be lying. Our records would prove it."

His voice sounded smoother than usual. "I'm with you, that the dinos didn't just up and go walkabout."

Portia's next words hurried out. "And I know that's a winner cow, and we've never granted a hunting permit for one. You have all you need to, how did you put it? Ring him up?"

The police inspector showed a callused palm. "We're on the right track, but we need more. Yes, doctor, you can tell a winner from a tina, but twelve random subjects of His Majesty? They'll want DNA evidence."

"Simple enough to provide," Portia said, but then a chill gripped her. How much DNA had survived taxidermy?

The cold sensation faded. She could research the matter online, or she could turn to the crime scene team. Police forensics techs must have more experience with extracting DNA from real-world samples than anyone.

"Our people would love to," Leichhardt said, "but they can't amplify dino DNA. Something about not having the, what are those doovalackies called? PCR primers for it. So we'll have to deputize the sequencing to your company."

"That shouldn't be a problem," Portia said, then wondered what she might've just committed the company to do.

His brown eyes fixed on her face. "Blockchain of custody is crucial. Martinson's lawyer will look for any moment when the samples left your sight between here and your DNA sequencing apparatus, in a bid to gin up reasonable doubt in a jury's mind. And your sequencing apparatus better have a proper maintenance history from the moment it rolled out of the fabricator."

"I understand."

"You're going to have to agree to share the inputs from your eyes and ears to your optic and auditory nerves through your neuronal interface into the planetary law enforcement blockchain. From the moment we hand you skin samples from the mounted dinos to the moment they enter your DNA sequencer. Do you agree?"

"I'll still be able to communicate privately through my neury?"

"If you don't speak out loud, yeah."

And with the information the company would provide the police, Martinson would face a penalty. The winner cow, and all the others, slain and skinned to make the cabinet of grotesqueries two levels below, would receive some justice. "Let's begin."

"Here's how you access the law enforcement blockchain." Leichhardt slipped his badge holder from his suit jacket's breast pocket. He flipped the badge up to reveal a QR code. "Run that through your neury."

She stared at the QR code until words formed in her vision. Black text crossed her view of flat-front cupboards. *Royal New New South Wales Law Enforcement Consortium Electronic Evidence Blockchain. You are hereby granted write-only access by Insp. Alan Leichhardt, Port Bounty PD, for the upload of personal audio and video recordings, relating to....*

Portia read the rest, then nodded. Her neury popped a winking red *REC* icon in the lower left corner of her vision, next to icons of a video camera and a microphone.

Leichhardt stood straight. "For the record, your name?"

"Portia Oakeshott. DVM."

"Your employer?"

"Blighland Dinosaur Preserve." Should she add the legal jargon at the back? "Proprietary Limited."

"Thank you, Dr. Oakeshott. I shall now take you to a location where we found evidence of a violation of Dinosaur Hunting Act 2749...."

Back to the lower basement. Amid the mounted bodies and body parts, Portia remained steadier on her feet. When she regarded the dead dinosaurs, the flipped minmi, the brightly-colored strallo, all the others, the winner cow's head most of all, dread and disgust were now alloyed with anger. The company's work—combining fossil evidence, bird DNA, educated guesswork, and Aussie pride—being exploited to serve some man's vanity—

The resident of this house had worked a vile crime, and she would do her part to make him pay.

Leichhardt introduced her to a forensics tech, a woman with tiny jowls and brown hair wisping out of a bun. "I'll cut and bag the samples," she said. Her voice was kindly and gritted by four or five decades of use. "How much do you need?"

"A picogram should be sufficient."

Wrinkles deepened around her eyes. "Field versus lab, and how much gets lost in tanning," she muttered to herself. "Got it."

The tech went from dinosaur to dinosaur, Portia in tow. With a whining rotary cutter, the tech cut one-centimeter squares of leatherized skin from the underside of each mounted figure. Each square went in a plastic baggie with an embedded RFID chip as the tech asked, "And this one is?"

Portia rattled off both the scientific and the common names, and each dinosaur's sex, if she could tell. The winner cow wasn't the only one that could not have been taken lawfully.

The tech nodded at each of Portia's identifications. When she had a sample, she sealed the square in its baggie and stared at the RFID chip. Portia's neury picked up the encoding of each chip by sounding a ding in her mind's ear and popping into her vision a call-out box with the dinosaur's identification and a timestamp. The tech clicked the rotary cutter's head into a handheld UV sterilizer as they went to the next mounted dinosaur.

"You've been in this line of work a while?" Portia asked over the hum of the sterilizer.

"Come back part-time after my youngest started primary school. Righty, now who's this bonzer bloke?"

They looked up at the winner cow. "That's a female winner. *Wintonotitan novacambrianovaaustraliensis.*" Portia's knees suddenly felt weak. She leaned her hand on the wall and sucked in a breath.

"Stay with me, doctor."

Portia drew in another breath, then nodded and stood tall again. "I remember, when I was a girl of five or six standard, we visited a couple who were friends of my parents. He hunted, not dinos, but the usual creatures stocked on Cookland. Emus, kangaroos. I wandered into his den and found a full roo mounted like—" She waved slender fingers at the minmi and the geiersaur.

"At first I thought it was a toy. Then I saw a bullethole in the chest and I thought the roo, he'd embalmed it, skin, flesh, bone, all, like the mummies on Pharaon." She shivered. "I had nightmares for weeks."

"It's just skin," the tech said.

"My father explained that to me...." Portia's legs wobbled again. Somewhere, a thousand kilometers to the south, lay a dead winner cow with its head skinned. Or had they skinned the entire carcass? She hadn't seen the resident's closet, how many leather jackets and pairs of cowboy boots had been made from the winner cow? Or, like they once did with elephants, had they turned her feet into meter-wide footstools?

The tech ducked under the placid head. She extended the rotary cutter to the underside of the winner's neck, where it met the wall. A brief whine, a zip as plastic sealed. The sounds grounded Portia back in the room. They moved on.

Though her legs felt steady, Portia avoided looking at the winner cow head as they finished their work.

After twenty minutes, they finished. The tech handed her a duffel bag marked *Property of PBPD*. All the samples inside barely weighted down the bag. Still, she trudged up the echoing concrete stairs. A young man so rich he could throw a monster party on a Twoday night, so scornful of the laws under which his family had prospered. It wasn't right. Not one bit.

She mulled these thoughts as another rideshare sedan took her, and the duffel bag on the seat next to her, out of the neighborhood. In places where the coast highway ran with only a guardrail between it and crashing waves, twilight glimmered to her left, a hair brighter than before. Maybe the weeks of winter made bad actors think darkness covered their crimes.

Actors. Plural. The spoiled rich resident of that house wouldn't have the skill or patience for taxidermy, too right.

After two kilometers eastward on the coast highway, toward the lighted highrises of downtown Port Bounty, the sedan turned right. Another two klicks brought her to the front gate of the company's campus. The gate recognized her and rose, allowing the rideshare in without stopping.

The sedan followed an asphalt lane flowing past sweetgums and oaks and along the terrain's contours to the main building. Blocks of quarried native stone gave the building an ancient dignity, like the public buildings seen in the background of a costume drama set in ancient Australia during the First World War. But the cameras and sensors tracking her entrance and the whisper of the doors sliding open for her approach were quite modern.

Portia carried the duffel bag over her shoulder to the wing of veterinary offices and labs. The sequencing lab hummed with machinery and air con. She shut the door behind her, then found the newest sequencer and checked its maintenance logs through her neury. As clean as the machine's molded plastic housing.

Satisfied, she got to work. The sequencer could handle eight samples at a time. Through her neury, she told the sequencer each sample's species and that it was tanned hide. Then she pressed *start*.

Lights flashed on the control panel and status messages crossed the screen. *Extracting DNA from leather... Determining species-specific primers... Amplification cycle 1....*

Ninety seconds later, the screen flicked to *Amplification cycle 2....*

Forty cycles of exponential duplication to get enough DNA for sequencing. Sequencing itself would be quick, but it would still take three sequencer runs to process all the samples.

Four hours later, the machine sounded a little fanfare. Final run complete. Data transferred to redundant and tamper-proof storage. Copied to the planet-wide police blockchain.

A message from Leichhardt de-deputized her. Gladly she stopped recording what she saw and heard. No journo she.

Freed, Portia requested a copy of the third run of sequences. She had a hunch from the first two runs, and wanted to see—

Knuckles rapped on the door.

"Come in," she called, expecting another veterinarian or a field ecologist.

The door opened. Portia's eyebrows jumped. Not a tech. Black hair low down his forehead, tailored gray suit accented with a bright yellow pocket square, body like a boxer from a light weight class. Pietrangelo, the company's chief operations officer.

Quickly she stood. "Mr. Pietrangelo, what brings you here?"

"I wanted to get a report from you. Had lunch? We'll hit the esky for some tucker."

"Sir, I..." She'd sat in the back of meetings he'd led, but in her three local years, six months standard, with the company, she'd never interacted with him face to face.

"On my quid. Come along." Not a command, exactly, but she followed without hesitation.

Pietrangelo strode down the corridors like a ship boosting at one *gee* for space far enough from stars and planets to enter hyperdrive. A powerful man. Portia pulled her arms closer. Her mother had warned her, powerful men could make a young lady devalue her virtue. But Pietrangelo's power flowed down proper channels, making the company run better, and protecting the dinosaurs on the preserve.

Didn't it?

The lunch room featured mass-produced plastic chairs and tables. One person, Alex the lead coder, ate alone. Veterinary director Hawkins and the other female vet, blond and sun-freckled Tiana Spence, broke off their conversation at the sight of Pietrangelo and hustled empty trays to the recycling hopper on their way out the door.

The esky, a cluster of storing, cooking, and serving modules, took up most of the back wall. No one waited at any of the order kiosks or tray dispensers. She went to the Mediterranean station, normally the most popular. Where was everyone? Her stomach growled and she double-checked the time. Nineteen o'clock, two hours after the main lunch hour at noon of New New South Wales' thirty-four hour day.

She sat near the window with a Greek salad, chicken shawarma, and hot tea steeping in a cup. Pietrangelo joined her, carrying a tray of spiced, orange-red meat grounds on lettuce boats and a mug of thick black coffee. Before he took his first bite, he asked, "Tell me what you've found so far."

"I've finished sequencing all twenty-three samples taken from the suspect's collection."

Muscles flexed at Pietrangelo's jaw hinges. He shook his head and spoke around a mouthful. "I saw that already. Have you looked at the data?"

"Yes. Who wouldn't?"

A swallow, then, "Notice anything?"

"Ten samples are from species we've never permitted for hunting. The winner, the—you've got the list?"

"Yeah. And I've checked records from the field offices. None of those species have crossed the perimeter since the suspect grew hair on his, ah, body."

"He took them on the preserve." Warmth filled her torso. "That's all the proof the police need."

Pietrangelo angled his head. "Probably, but tell me more."

"The snips showing where we released their founding generations are almost all from the sector near the town of Blenheim."

Pietrangelo regarded her in silence for a moment. Her mouth turned dry. Had she made a mistake?

Snips—single nucleotide polymorphisms—existed in nature because of the genetic code's redundancy. Some random mutations left intact the function of an encoded protein. In human and natural animal populations, snips served as markers of ethnicity and—her cheeks warmed—paternity.

When the company raised a stock of eggs and hatchlings for release, the genetic engineers created sets of snips encoding data relating to that stock. Among that encoded data, time and place of release into the preserve. She'd double-checked the data extracted by the sequencer against the company's records. Near the town of Blenheim. No doubt.

"*Almost* all?"

"The only exception was a geiersaur, released in the next sector, south of Margarettown."

"And the only flier." Pietrangelo reached for his coffee. "One might call that a clue."

Tension bled from Portia's shoulders. "The suspect hunted in the sector near Blenheim," she said, voice bright. "And that's where the police should look for the taxidermist."

"Good thought." Pietrangelo lifted a lettuce boat of spiced meat.

Coriander, cumin? Portia's nose couldn't tell. "You can talk about it with them."

Puzzlement wrinkled the skin between her eyes. "I've told Inspector Leichhardt all I know."

"I'm certain of that, but Blenheim is a thousand klicks out of his jurisdiction. We've called in the Royal Frontier Police."

Portia's eyes went wide. "The frontos?"

"Think that's what I said. And in fact—" Pietrangelo turned his head. She read the gesture as him checking something through his neury. "Oh bugger, he's early." He crammed another lettuce boat into his mouth in two bites, then grabbed his mug of black coffee by the handle. "Come along, doctor. You can bring your tea."

Portia carried her half-full tray to the recycler with one hand, her cuppa with the other. Pietrangelo stalked through the halls to the elevators. She hurried to keep up.

His office filled a corner of the top floor. Dimly visible through reflections in the windows were the racked lights of skycrapers downtown on one side and the campus' hatcheries and utility buildings on the other.

A man with broad shoulders waited in a leather-upholstered chair in front of Pietrangelo's wide, true-wood desk. The stranger wore brown hair close to his scalp, and Portia couldn't decide if he had enough stubble on his jaw and chin to call it a beard. He had bags under his eyes. From the outdated cut and color palette, his slacks, shirt, and vest could have come from the same tailor as her father.

He stood up. The badge flipped open at his vest pocket flashed a reflection at her eyes. "G'day. Special Agent Lamar Dowling, RFP." The flow of his voice made her revise his age downward. Thirty standard. "Hope you don't mind, the expert system, artificial personality, whatever you call your virtual assistant let me in to wait."

"No worries," Pietrangelo said, and introduced himself. They shook hands like they were trying to crush each other's bones. Men.

With a wince, Pietrangelo broke off the handshake. "And this is Dr. Portia Oakeshott."

Dowling blinked heavily as he reached for her hand. He gripped it softly, with skin smoother than she expected. "Ph.D.?"

"DVM."

"Ripper. Wouldn't want to go on this trip with someone whose nose is up near the top of her ivory tower."

Portia bristled. Then frowned. "Trip?"

Dowling raised an eyebrow at Pietrangelo. "What have you told her?"

"Not much. She figured it out on her own." He went around his desk, to a chair with keypad-laden arms like those Portia imagined graced the bridge of a hyperdrive ship. "Everyone, have a seat."

She took one of the leather chairs facing the desk, Dowling the other. Though her skirt was hemmed at mid-calf, she kept her knees together and pointed away from the Frontier Police agent and twisted her upper body to face him. "You're going after the taxidermist."

Dowling turned his baggy eyes to her gaze. "And others, too. Our laired-up bastard took all the dinos from the same part of the preserve, right? Makes me think he's got helpers in or around Blenheim. Any guesses what kind of help they're giving him?"

"A tracker, perhaps? And a pilot. Someone with that much money wouldn't take ten or twelve hours to drive across Blighland when a charter aircraft could make the run in two. Wait, the pilot would be based here."

"Good thoughts." He peered at her, expecting more.

But what? Muscles bunched around her mouth... and then she remembered she wasn't at uni any more. These men weren't professors grading her. "A policeman can think of more than I can, I'm sure."

Special Agent Dowling bowed his head at the compliment. "Here's a big one that hadn't occurred to you. Where's the rest of the winner?"

The bridge of her nose wrinkled. "Somewhere in the preserve... where a field team might stumble on it? He dragged it off the preserve? No, the cameras didn't see it."

"My guess would be he buried it," said Dowling, "and that would take the devil's own long time with a shovel. He probably used a bulldozer."

"One can't sneak a bulldozer past the perimeter cameras," Portia said. Then her gaze darted to Pietrangelo. "Can one?"

Pietrangelo ran fingers between his neck and his shirt collar. "No, but we have bulldozers on the preserve, in the utility sheds at Hocknull Lodge."

"He broke into our facility?" Portia couldn't believe it. The way Pietrangelo scowled at his coffee mug, and a world-weary expression flickered over Dowling's face, showed they didn't believe it either.

Her blood ran cold. With wobbly hands, she set her cuppa down on the desk before she spilled it. "A company employee helped him?"

"It's a possibility we have to consider," Pietrangelo said. "If we've got a bad apple, I want to make a corker of an example of him to the other employees."

"And I'm looking for every angle I can to make a run at our suspect," added Dowling.

His words barely registered. She blinked around heat building around her eyes. "Of course," she said, more mildly than she felt. An employee flouting the company's mission.... She sniffed in a breath. Change your train of thought. "Special Agent, I see the need for you to investigate at Blenheim and Hocknull Lodge, but why do you want me on your trip?"

"I need a dino expert. We might have remains to identify, DNA to sequence, that sort of thing."

"I'm flattered," she said. She turned to Pietrangelo. "But many people here have more experience than I do. I've never been to Blenheim or Hocknull...." Her eyes widened.

Satisfaction sparked in Pietrangelo's dark eyes. "You're a sharp one, Dr. Oakeshott."

Dowling scratched the stubble on his jaw. "We'll go undercover. Perhaps as a tourist couple. I'll work up a story. Maybe newlyweds—"

Portia clamped her knees more tightly together and pointed them further away from the Frontier Police agent.

"—relax, doctor. Whenever I marry, it won't be to a wowser."

Her back stiffened. "I'm not a wowser." She knew how to have fun without a gutful of alcohol or a casual root.

Dowling rolled his eyes. "Can we book a two-room suite at the lodge?" he asked Pietrangelo.

"The suites are almost always booked far in advance. I can't pull the rug out from under a paying customer. You can try to reserve a suite right now, though it's buckley's chance one's available."

"I don't know when we'll get to the lodge," Dowling said. "We might not even visit the lodge at all. If we do, if a standard room has a couch long enough, that'll do me. Will that suffice, doctor?" Sarcasm spiced his last words.

She arched an eyebrow at him. "Barely."

Special Agent Dowling barked out a laugh. "You're a dinkum sheila, doctor."

Portia kept her eyebrow raised until Pietrangelo's pensive expression came through to her. "Sir?"

"We don't open the preserve to tourists till the day before vernal equinox," he said in his firm voice to Dowling. "2nd of Spring this year."

"Eight days from now." Dowling scratched his stubbly brown beard. "Word of the suspect's arrest will get out by then. His associates will cover their tracks, maybe even blow town. Any way to get down there now?"

"We do construction and maintenance work during the off-season. We can book you as contractors."

"It's got to be something that gives us an excuse to stay in Blenheim, if that's where the clues go."

"Too right," said Pietrangelo. "If I heard a contractor is blodging around off the preserve, I'd sack them immediately."

A hush descended. Portia picked up her cuppa from the desk. When she raised it to her lips, a thought worked loose. "Tourism consultants. The company hired us to review all aspects of the visitor experience, from the moment tourists step off the plane till they check out from the lodge."

Dowling's eyebrows quirked. "Clever. You sure you want to do this dino thing, Dr. Oakeshott? You might have a knack for police work."

Portia blinked. Images of mounted dinosaurs flashed on the inside of her eyelids. A tremble ran through her arms but thank God her tea stayed in its cup.

She swallowed around a tiny lump in her throat. "Veterinary work is the only job for me."

CHAPTER 2

The panels overhead tried to give the aircraft's passengers the full spectrum of summer sunlight, but a glance out the windows dispelled the feeling. They flew through darkness, away from a dim smear of twilight, above a hidden landscape where the solitary lights of isolated farmsteads shone like lighthouses.

A spike of air pressure in Portia's ear informed her of their descent to Blenheim. The flap motors whined in the wings. The lights of the town filled the windows on the right. A small place, perhaps five thousand souls, but after overflying a thousand klicks of empty land, Blenheim seemed to stretch on like the glow of Endeavour Bay and New Canberra all rolled into one.

Tires chirped on asphalt. The landing jostled her against her shoulder belt. The engines hummed to slow them down, giving her a usual instant of worry that they'd overshoot the end of the runway. But the plane slowed and turned smoothly onto the taxiway, to the sighs and yawns of the half-dozen other passengers in the mostly empty cabin.

Dowling sat taller, which straightened some of the wrinkles in his size-too-big jacket. Zippers and carabiners clanked and clinked. He rubbed his baggy eyes. Around a yawn, he said, "I miss anything?"

"Bog standard descent," she said. "You slept solidly."

"Habit I learned in the Defense Force. Sleep when you can."

Her eyes widened. "You've been off-planet?"

"Days in one metal can followed by weeks in a larger one. The devil's own lack of glamour, let me tell you."

"But, you traveled in space...."

He laughed lightly. "I was military police stationed at Black Stump." A can-world, orbiting a gas giant, Watson, a billion kilometers away. Black Stump served as the main transshipment point for hyperdrive ships entering and leaving the Stella Australis system. "Spent most of my time tossing drunks into the back of the divvy van."

The aircraft rolled to the terminal. She glanced out the window and worry needled her. No other planes waited.... because she'd just arrived at a small town about a week before the tourist season. This wasn't Endeavour Bay's airport, with scores of departures and arrivals every day. She was lucky Blenheim had paved the runway.

Down a concourse lined with a tea kiosk, a fish-and-chips esky, the flashing lights of a gambling room, and a gift shop festooned with inaccurately-depicted stuffed dinosaurs. Behind the counters, bored girls chewed gum. Eyes ringed with too much makeup had the vacant looks of people engrossed by their neuries. Near the terminal exits, a skycap and his team of wheeled robots offered to carry their luggage to their car.

"Follow me," Dowling said. They went out the sliding doors.

Damp, chill air struck Portia's face. She hunched her shoulders and pulled in her neck. Thin fog diffused globular streetlights, shining at full power an hour before noon.

The special agent must have arranged their ride through his neury: a dark gray ute on raised tires rolled to the curb. It popped its doors. She climbed in while Dowling chatted with the skycap. Smells of leather and new car. She sat in one of the bucket seats in the rear. The robots slid their luggage into the ute's bed, next to the extended range battery under a rigid plastic tonneau cover. The skycap and his machines then returned to the warmth and light of the terminal.

Dowling joined her in the cabin, taking one of the rear-facing seats across from her. Ten centimeters separated their knees. Accent lights on the underside of the seats gave the cabin a cozy feeling. Portia pressed her knees together and angled them to the side. The ute shut its doors and rolled away from the terminal.

To say something, she asked, "Is this ute fronto standard issue?"

His seat back still adjusted to fit his broad shoulders. "No, I rented it as part of our cover."

"I hope I have it straight. We're pretending we're secret shoppers hired by the local tourism board, who are pretending they're a rich couple from Cookland?"

"Ripper."

"Can we practice more at the hotel?"

"We don't have time. It's already been thirty hours since I've gotten on the case. The taxidermist who mounted the winner cow and the other dinos might already have poured bleach and shone ultraviolet light on every square centimeter of his work area. If we wait till check-in time at the hotel, then practice, the local taxidermists will've closed up shop for the day, and we won't have a chance to question them till tomorrow morning. We've got to go now."

Portia fell silent. The ute traveled a two-lane road between a tobacco farm under growlights and a paddock of riddlepigs. "I'm not good at lying."

"You'll do fine, doctor."

Three taxidermists plied their trade in Blenheim. All looked the same from the outside: low buildings dressed in local stone, metal roofs, parking lots of gravel looking gray under security lights. Likewise inside. Sun-spectrum ceiling panels shown on lobbies with extruded plastic furniture, video frames looping outdoors scenes from the weeks of summer, and the stuffed full-sized skins of roos, pet dogs, and grackelsaurs.

Dowling played a hunter, come down from Cookland to meet and hire a guide for four days in Latesummer. With subtle shifts of voice, face, and posture, he looked and sounded ten years older and many fold richer. The grizzled men behind the counters, wearing thick aprons stained by chemicals, and not enough cologne to mask the odor of tanning agents, gave Portia appraising looks from the hem to the neck of her fitted dress, from mid-calf to collarbones.

The first time, after a moment of shock, she defiantly stood taller and canted her hip closer to Dowling. In the next two interviews, she put on the pose coming right out the gate. In all cases, the men glanced away from her and focused on Dowling with added respect.

Ten minutes with the first man, then the special agent thanked him and led Portia out. After the ute closed its doors and gravel crunched under the tires, she asked, "How can you tell it wasn't him?"

Dowling scratched his brown stubble. "I haven't been to church on a regular basis for many years, but there's a line that applies to my line of work. 'The guilty fleeth when no man pursueth.'"

Now that she had an inkling what to look for, the second man struck her as innocent from the start. A talkative old-timer, rambling about hunters he'd seen, reminiscing about the earliest days of the preserve; but an expert at how best to process the hides of the different dinosaur species commonly brought to him by hunters.

"What about a winner?" Dowling asked casually.

"Ha'n't a clue. The company have never let any hunter take one."

Dowling shrugged his broad shoulders. "Just 'cause the company've never permitted it...."

"If a hunter's ever poached one, he never brought it to me to mount."

"Small wonder," Dowling said. "It'd take an eighteen-wheel flatbed to get it here."

"Too right," said the old man. "Though I remember, back in '53, one young bastard and his mates got the wobbly on and decided to sneak into the preserve and bag a tino. They stumbled upon a clutch of stralla eggs." He chuckled. "Then the stralla caught their scent. Those boys ran for their lives like jumbucks...."

The old man still chuckled as Dowling and Portia took their leave.

The third taxidermist's reception area had brighter sun-spectrum lights than the other two. A dusty minmi head stared down from above a mottled gray, synthetic stone counter. In a corner near the minmi's head, a smoke-brown wart covered a surveillance camera.

When Dowling tapped the bell on the counter, a man shuffled out of the work area. Silver hair, thin on top but brushing his shoulders. In Portia's hometown, she would have interpreted his hairstyle as that of a professional with a high-rise office taking up some rough-and-tumble hobby during a midlife crisis. She couldn't tell what it might mean around here. Certainly, no professional in an office would leave so much nostril hair in his turned-up nose.

With a booming yet guarded voice, the taxidermist asked, "How can I help ya?"

"Have a minute?" Dowling said. "I don't want to tie you up if you're busy."

"Nah, it's the slow season."

Portia briefly squinted at the man's clean workshirt. His cologne was as thick the others', but without any need for it. She inhaled quietly and caught only traces of chemicals from the work area out back. His season was slower than the others'.

"I'm down from Cookland," Dowling said, "scouting for a hunting trip coming up in three weeks. Looking for the lay of the land, meeting blokes I can work with, that sort of thing."

The silver-haired man's voice brightened. "You'll need taxidermy, then. What are you going after?"

"Dinos."

A quick nod. "I can do dinos."

"Good. Yeah, I was thinking about... winners."

The taxidermist blinked rapidly and his head jittered. He regained his composure, fixing wide eyes on Dowling and darting his head forward and back about five centimeters at a time.

The special agent dipped his chin in a single nod. With portentious ease he turned to Portia. "Be a love and turn off your neury."

She scowled at him while her thoughts raced. What would some superficial woman do? Like Tiana Spence, lunching yesterday with her and Portia's male boss. "I'm watching a very important story."

"Oh?"

"Princess Julia was seen at a gala in New Can last night. Her skirt was hemmed two centimeters above the knee." When Dowling said nothing, she said. "Above the knee! When we get home, you'll have to buy me an entire new wardrobe."

Dowling gave her a smile that reached his eyes, though she wished it hadn't. "Home is four thousand klicks away. Turn off your damned neury."

If he tired of law enforcement, he could find work as an actor playing villains. Her eyelids fluttered. She ducked her gaze. One last ping before she turned off her neury told her Dowling had powered down his too.

The taxidermist looked between the two of them. He licked his lips and nodded. "There's no microphone in here, but—" He rolled his eyes up and back, in the direction of the surveillance camera. "—watch that your lips might get read."

"I can talk like this," Dowling said. He didn't mumble but his lips barely moved. Forget acting, he could do ventriloquy. "And lovey's not going to say a word. Right, lovey?"

Portia swallowed thickly. Her head bobbed up and down.

The taxidermist's voice boomed. "You want a winner, you said?"

"Would that be a problem?"

"The dino company doesn't give winner permits."

Dowling's smile bared teeth. "I'm aware of that. If I need a winner mounted, would that be a problem?"

"No, no. Not at all. I've got a lot of experience—"

"With winners?" Dowling's voice dripped doubt.

The taxidermist opened his mouth, then leaned back. His eyes narrowed. "Are you johnny law? You have to tell me the truth, 'cause if you lie, the rest of this conversation is, what do they call it, in-trap-mint."

Dowling pivoted his head to Portia. "He's never done a winner. Come along, lovey. We'll figure this out another way." He turned his shoulders to face her, excluding the taxidermist.

"Good," Portia said. "I can get back to my video about Princess Julia."

The special agent laid a hand on her upper arm and directed her torso to turn toward the door. They each took a step—

"Wait," said the taxidermist. His words came out in a desperate flood. "You're right, mate, I've never mounted a winner. But I've done other dinos, how hard can it be? You wouldn't have to bring in a bloke from Port Bounty or nothing."

Dowling stopped. He turned his broad shoulders like an ocean-going cargo ship slowly changing bearing to enter the harbor at Endeavour Bay. "Which bloke?"

The taxidermist shook his head, as if flicking the question off the tip of his up-turned nose. "I'll charge a better price. Plus you don't have to pay for my flight down or a room to flop."

"Or a truck big enough to drive a winner's corpse here."

"Yeah, that too, mate, of course." The taxidermist grinned like a child hoping a strict parent would indulge him with candy.

"Plus," Dowling said, "Port Bounty's a big place. I wouldn't know where to look for him."

"And you can always find me here."

Dowling's baggy eyes regarded the silver-haired man. "I'll keep you in mind. G'day."

After the crunch of gravel gave way to the whisper of asphalt, a grin creased Dowling's face. "That makes a heck of a lot of sense, doesn't it? The suspect's got the devil's own pile of quid. He can hire the best taxidermist in Port Bounty."

"Or any of the bigger cities on Cookland," Portia said.

"You've the hang of this, doctor. Fly down the man and his supplies, put him up in a hotel.... So the taxidermist from the big smoke cools his heels at the hotel while the suspect sneaks onto the preserve, poaches a dino, and brings back the skin or as much of the carcass as will fit on a truck."

A limp bit of neck and sightless head of a winner draped across one of two queen beds in a bog standard room, with blood still dripping. " Not to the hotel."

"Ripper. Did he bring the taxidermist with him? Mount the skins in the field? How much equipment would the taxidermist need to bring with him?"

Portia shook her head. Her imagination suddenly flashed to the winner cow, shot through the chest, long neck collapsing.

Dowling went on. "Too much equipment and too much time to mount the skin out on the preserve. And you're right, he didn't do it in a hotel. The suspect must've set up his hired taxidermist in a building somewhere."

It was a small town, yet, "There must be quite a number of suitable buildings here in Blenheim," Portia said.

"And thousands of barns and sheds on farms between here and the preserve." The ute slowed and turned into the hotel's nearly empty parking lot. They parked near the front doors and climbed out. Bright globular streetlights at the corners of the lot cast X-shaped shadows on the asphalt.

An hour later, after they checked into their adjoining rooms and Portia unpacked and changed clothes, they met in the hotel's restaurant for a late lunch. A plush red rope blocked off a darkened half of the dining area. A solitary waiter, a stiff-backed boy fresh out of school, with more acne than whiskers on his face, took their orders, then returned with their two cups of tea.

"I did some research into taxidermy just now," Portia said. "You're right, it couldn't have been performed on site. There's too much equipment to feasibly drive onto the preserve. Chemicals to clean the skins, wire and foam to construct a mannequin, and the tools to work those materials. And even with modern tech, the process takes at least a day, and more like three or four if the taxidermist wants his work to qualify as a handicraft." She poured sweetened milk in her tea and sipped.

"We could go knock on five thousand doors looking for their worksite," Dowling said. "That obviously won't go."

"I trust you're thinking aloud," Portia asked. "I'm not a policewoman."

Dowling chuckled. "That's how I work. Like a scientist. I kick around hypotheses that fit what we know, then do research to test them."

Portia raised her eyebrows. Her image of frontos had the square-jawed, but somewhat dim, heroes of cartoons and action movies baked in. "You're not what I expected from a Frontier Policeman."

"And how many frontos have you ever met, doctor?" He spoke lightly.

She reached for her tea to mask a warmth on her cheeks and give her gaze an excuse to drop from his eyes. Though she was no more than ten standard years younger than him, she felt like a naïve girl.

The special agent's voice took on a down-to-business tone. "We need more leads. I called our regional office in Port Bounty and head-quarters in New Can, to see if any prominent taxidermists have made repeated trips down here. I also enquired about any real estate the suspect or his family might own in the area. No word yet."

Portia sipped more from her cuppa. "I don't want to wait around the hotel till they get back to you."

"We won't. But why don't you want to wait?"

The squeak of the waiter's trainers on the hardwood floor heralded the arrival of their lunch. For her, hydroponic greens and cherry tomatoes strewn with slices of seared tuna and drizzled with a balsamic vinaigrette. She knifed greens and a protein slice into a dainty bite, and hesitated with the fork near her mouth. If she weren't careful talking about her feelings, she'd make herself sick. "Martinson needs to be punished for what he did."

Dowling swallowed a mouthful of cheeseburger. "You're a loyal employee," he said.

She could tell from his voice that he intentionally said something he didn't believe, but she couldn't stop herself from speaking harshly. "I'm not angry for the company's interests. I'm angry about those dinos he slaughtered."

"You don't like hunting."

Portia jammed the forkful of salad into her mouth. She chewed vigorously, glad to have an excuse to delay her answer. After swallowing, she said, "I don't like killing anything, especially the dinos, but I know there's a purpose for it. Managing herd numbers to stay within carrying capacity, balancing our interests against those of our neighbors...." She squeezed her eyes shut for a moment, drew a breath. "Hunting's part of the circle of life. But what he did? He knew he had no right to shoot the winner and every other dino he poached and he did it anyway." She hissed out the final words.

Sometime while she spoke, Dowling had rested his cheeseburger on his plate. He regarded her with his baggy eyes. "You've got a lot of fire in your belly for this case. That's good. But keep it under control."

"Why?" she asked. Her sharp tone of voice wasn't like her at all. She took a breath and said, much more properly, "Oh, for evidence and police procedure reasons."

"Those too."

She blinked. "What am I missing, special agent?"

"When you kick over rocks, you never know when you'll surprise a venomous snake."

Portia pulled her arms closer to her ribs. "The suspect is in custody, isn't he?"

"His father bailed him out. The judge ordered him to remain in Port Bounty or the neighboring shire. But I'm not talking about the suspect or the taxidermist. The suspect had local help. Someone provided him the bulldozer to bury the winner's corpse, right? Others might have been involved, too."

"If we find the local help, they might turn violent? Why?"

"Ten counts of dinosaur poaching could be punished with a sizable amount of personality modification and a fine that would garnish half a workingman's wages for a century. And a man who breaks one law tends to break others. The punishment for all his crimes might go well beyond what he's already facing. Escaping that might in his mind justify violence. And a man living a life of crime tends to act impulsively to begin with."

"I'll be careful."

"Good," Dowling said with a trace of affection.

Portia's head snapped up. Did he harbor an attraction for her? The look in his baggy eyes and the outdated style of his jacket showed otherwise. Affectionate like an uncle, not an aspiring boyfriend.

Muscles in her face eased. The greens and reds on her plate made her want to wolf them down. "What, then, is our plan for the rest of the day?"

"We find the building where Lachlan Martinson set up the taxidermist."

Her eyebrows rose. "We'll knock on five thousand doors?"

Dowling laughed. "No. Just one."

CHAPTER 3

The real estate agent's office filled the front half of the middle floor of a five-story building in downtown Blenheim. A planter box crowded with greenery ran the width of the room, in front of floor-to-ceiling windows behind her desk. Leafy and earthy smells, moist from drip irrigation, filled the room. The windows faced across the street the shire council office, a building crowned with stone towers topped with finials. Too massive a building for its city block. Beyond the council office, light glowed on the northwestern horizon.

Portia frowned. Too bright to be winter twilight this far south. She pointed. "What's all that?"

The real estate agent looked that way and blinked eyes with long lashes. Vanessa Wilford, said the name laser-etched on the glass door. She spoke with a voice that tried to be chummy but failed. "That's the ancient British history museum." Portia had lived in Port Bounty long enough to recognize her accent as being from that city.

Dowling acted the part of the crass rich man. "This town's a hell of an odd place for one."

A naughty thrill ran through Portia at the swear word. *Wait, you're pretending to be a rich man's kept woman, and your knickers are in a twist over **hell**?*

"Blenheim is named after the ancestral estate of some names you might have heard of." Wilford ticked them off on long fingers. "The Duke of Marlborough, Winston Churchill, Princess Diana. And the museum's symbolic of why I, and many others, have moved here. Sit, please. Tea?"

"I'll take a cuppa," Portia said.

Dowling shook his head, lips pursed. "Which is?"

The real estate agent pressed the buttons on the billy. Hot steam carried the scent of Earl Grey to Portia's nose.

Wilford turned back to Dowling. "Opportunity. My husband and I moved down in '64."

Portia blinked. From the woman's wavy black hair and the dusting of freckles on her smooth cheeks, all seen under the sharp glare of sun-spectrum ceiling panels, she'd guessed the real estate agent to be two decades younger.

"The town might have had five hundred residents, all living within a few blocks of the original council office." Wilford waved long fingers toward the window. "But we knew the dinosaur preserve would bring in tourists, and tourists would inspire people to further development, like the museum. More development would mean more jobs, would mean high wages to attract workers from up north, would mean high demand for real estate."

Dowling said, "I take it you've done well enough to justify leaving Port Bounty all those years ago."

"Well enough." Wilford handed Portia a recyclable cup, then sat behind her desk. She swiveled her chair to face Dowling. "How can I help you?"

"I'm looking to buy a country getaway. Someplace secluded, between here and the dino preserve. We'd come down during the summer and rent out the land to a riddlepig farmer or—"

"Pigs?" On cue, Portia wrinkled her nose. "Don't they put up a horrid stink?"

Dowling gave her an indulgent smile masking a sharp edge. "You paying any quid for this, lovey?"

With a quiet clearing of her throat, Wilford brought their attention back to her. "More and more sophisticated people are discovering the quiet joys of a country getaway. We have a good number of properties that could meet your needs."

"I knew Lackey gave us a dinkum reco."

A smile pushed up the freckles on Wilford's cheeks, though confusion touched her eyes. "Word of mouth is the best advert," she said, "but which 'Lackey' do you mean?"

Portia's heart pounded. They were taking a flyer, that Martinson had sought out the one real estate agent in town whose public bio spoke of growing up in Port Bounty, when he needed to find a base for his poaching.

"Lachlan Martinson," Dowling said. "He's a young bloke from Port Bounty. I met him a few years back, at a hunting lodge in the north Cookland bush."

Wilford's mouth quirked at the name before she forced her smile wider. "Of course. I went to secondary school with his father."

"You helped him find a 'country place,' but I couldn't tell if he meant a farm spread or a place in town."

"A farm. Very much like what you want, except he wanted a rental rather than a place for sale. A good way out of town. The back paddocks border the dino preserve."

Portia's breath caught. She clawed her way back into character and rolled her eyes. "I suppose dinos stink less than riddlepigs."

"She's telling us what Lackey got, lovey, not what I want." He angled his head and one eyebrow crept up. "Not necessarily." To Wilford, he said, "You have the address?"

Portia stamped her foot. "You *cannot* be serious. Bad enough you only want to be seen in public with me in a woop woop town thousands of klicks from anyone who might know you have a—"

"Lovey." Dowling's voice knifed through the room.

Portia quailed. On the other hand, after Wilford returned her attention from her neury, she gave the special agent a look of cougarish appraisal. With a husk in her voice, she said, "21 Shire Road 79-58."

"Half an hour in our ute?"

"Closer to an hour. The farm is on a gravel road over twenty klicks east of the main highway to the dino preserve."

"We'll run by on our way to check out some other properties you might be able to give us."

"Of course. I have a good number of places that might fit your needs. It will help if you give me a price range."

With a wince in his baggy eyes, the special agent said, "I can't go too high. What would a million quid get me?"

Wilford blinked at Dowling, then swept black hair behind her ear with her long fingers. "You'll be spoiled for choice...."

Portia and Special Agent Dowling left the real estate office twenty minutes later, with a list of five properties located between Blenheim and the preserve. Wilford offered to ride out with them, saying to Dowling while ignoring Portia, "My husband and I've no plans for the evening, he won't mind if I show you."

"We'll take a look around on our own, then get back in touch when we're ready to make an offer on one." Dowling put on a courteous smile which stayed on his face until the ute pulled up to the curb and they climbed in. The leather of the rear seats crinkled under her. Dowling sat opposite her, at the front of the cabin, facing the rear. The doors thumped shut before he said, "I wouldn't want to be the unlucky bastard married to her."

"I thought a woman her age would have outgrown the urge to flirt."

Dowling chortled. "The wonders of modern medicine. Never mind that. We've got a lead."

"Your hunch panned out."

"I figured Martinson would want to play things close to the vest. Shire Road 79-58, here we come."

The ute worked its way through downtown Blenheim and to the main southbound road. Cars and other utes crowded the road near fish-and-chips and pizza takeaways, pubs, and a city park with a well-lit footy pitch.

Why so much traffic? She checked the time through her neury and blinked in surprise. Already twenty-four o'clock, the end of the work-day. Between their late lunch and the lack of even an hour of twilight, she'd lost track of time.

Which ticked by as the ute hummed its way down the asphalt two-lane, into the even deeper darkness of the south polar winter evening. The town and its glowing lights thinned out. Side roads branched off on both sides. Wide, asphalted, and frequent at first, by ten klicks south of Blenheim, the side roads were gravel gouges a lane-and-a-half wide, running due east-west, hitting the highway about two klicks apart. Only the signs posting them as shire roads made them seem anything more than farmers' driveways.

Between the side roads, fences ran along the two-lane. The only turnouts led to farmhouses set a thousand meters off the road, or wireless comms towers.

When the ute passed Shire Road 79-54, the numbering suddenly made sense. "That's latitude, isn't it? 79°54' south?"

"You've got it. Don't drive around here much?"

"We get around in quaddies, usually."

Dowling said nothing, but Portia suddenly felt spoiled. She lowered her gaze a moment. "You frontos spend a lot of time in ground vehicles?"

"Yeah, but I also know the region I'm working."

"I've only been with the company three local years!" She hugged her arms to her sides. "You needn't be judgmental."

"I wasn't," Dowling said mildly. "Should I've been? Are you one of those?"

"One of those what?"

"A city slicker who thinks the millions of data shufflers in the big smoke matter and rural folk in woop woop towns don't?"

Portia felt chill. She managed to say, "I only called Blenheim a woop woop town to stay in character..."

Dowling raised his hand, palm-out. "You did well. And I want you to remember something. To the folk around here, the corner of Dinosaur Preserve Highway and Shire Road 79-58 is as important as the corner of Coronation and Bourke in downtown Endeavour Bay."

She'd been there. After graduation, she'd taken the tube downtown with her parents for dinner at a ninetieth-floor restaurant looking out on the rippling bay. To get to the restaurant from the tube station, they'd walked crowded sidewalks and crossed the street at the most famous intersection on the planet. Thousands of footsteps, thousands of electric car motors humming, all echoing down urban canyons walled with steel, glass, and carbon nanotube alloys. Unease had tempered her jubilant mood. One young woman in one large city. Would real life fulfill all her dreams from uni?

The young women, and young men, and the children, the middle-aged, the elderly of both sexes from around here had dreams too, and the challenge to fulfill them.

"Thank you. I hadn't thought of that."

"Come to think of it, I want you to remember something else. When your dad gets his new, cloned liver out of a riddlepig, or your mum one-ups the rest of her bridge club by bringing a bottle of the trendiest new syrah, they can do those things because of rural folk in woop woop towns."

"My dad doesn't drink that much...." That wasn't the point. "I shouldn't take the people around here for granted."

Dowling grinned. "I'll make a fronta of you yet, Dr. Oakeshott." The ute slowed. The special agent craned his neck. "I reckon here's our turn."

The ute's headlights swept over the sign for Shire Road 79-58. Gravel rattled under the wheels. Washboard ripples shook the ute. Ahead, the gravel road ran straight, up and down rolls in the terrain, as far as the headlights could illuminate. Farmhouses and comms towers stood in dark fields. Barbed-wire fences flanked the road. Behind them grazed riddlepigs, sheep sheared for natural wool, ranches of free-range cattle, hunting parks stocked with emus. More than she had imagined.

Something else came to mind. "The farm rented by Lachlan Martinson is on this road? And its back fence is at the outer perimeter of the dinosaur preserve?"

"Both."

The crown grant of land for the preserve began at 80° south. A minute of latitude on New New South Wales was about one kilometer. "The farm is two klicks from front to back?"

"And two wide. Standard for this area."

"We'll have to go on site to investigate."

"Eventually, yes. First we'll drive by. We can do that without a warrant."

The ute rolled on. A combination of washboarded road and the crest of a terrain roll jostled her so hard the seatbelt tensed, the shoulder strap too tight across her chest. By the time she unbuckled and rebuckled with a little slack, Dowling's head lolled back. He breathed slowly and his baggy eyes were closed.

When you get a chance to sleep, take it. *Wake me five minutes before we get to Number 21*, she told her neury. After one last look at the dark farmland on both sides of the ute, she shut her eyes, doubting she'd fall asleep.

A glow inside her eyelids and a bonging in her ears roused her. Her neury told her the ute approached Number 19, the farm adjacent their target. Narrow steel fenceposts, each painted white and one-meter-fifty tall, lined the roadside like soldiers at attention. Taut barbed wire stretched between them. Portia expected black or gray cattle to be grazing in the field behind the fences, but she couldn't see them in the polar gloom.

The barbed wire fence curved away from the roadside at the entrance to a narrow gravel lane. No gate, just a set of pipes running laterally across the top of a trench the width of the lane. During her livestock training, she'd learned the pipe-and-trench structure was called a cattle guard.

A sign rising up from the last fencepost before the curve bore red paint artistically announcing *One Family Under God—The Yeardleys*. Five meters behind and to the far side of the gate rose a plain white cross, six or eight meters tall and gleaming in the glow of ground-mounted floodlights.

Dowling blinked at the giant cross, then bowed his head to Portia. "Now that's a wowser. I'll never call you one again."

He reached into his jacket and pulled out an object barely larger than the last joint of his thumb. His trimmed fingernails pried at something. In the dim light, his baggy eyes scowled. "I'm not having luck. You have a go, doctor."

The special agent extended his arms. Into her palm he dropped the object. A black plastic disc, two centimeters in diameter and one thick.

A white strip ringed the disc near the circumference on one side. "A go at...?"

"The adhesive backing."

A pair of glassy circles stared out of the disc. Camera lenses. "Ah." Portia worked her fingernail into a seam in the backing and peeled it off. She cradled it in her fingers, sticky- and camera-side up, and handed it back.

Dowling took it, twisted in his seat, and pressed it to a lower corner of the ute's side window. Portia could barely see it next to the health and safety stickers she hadn't noticed.

"I'll share the camera feed to your neury," Dowling said.

"How much can a camera see in the dark?"

"A good bit. Night vision. Image processing."

She accessed the camera. Her neury showed her a greenish augmented reality overlay on her view out the window. Distant dots, glowing on four legs, were the Yeardley's cattle.

The ute rolled on. A minute after passing the Yeardleys' front gate, the straight white fenceposts were replaced by thicker ones, two meters tall, of unpainted steel. A helix of razor wire crested the top of the new fence, angled in.

She shivered. No family farm, this. That fence could better keep out a boomer, a full-grown male kangaroo... except the razor wire coil aimed to keep something *in*. But Dowling's camera showed only rolling ground tufted with unkempt grasses, with no animal visible. In the distance, a grove of trees covered a low ridge. Her neury estimated the range to the grove at fifteen hundred meters.

"The whole back paddock is out of sight from the road," Dowling said.

The ute soon came to the entrance to Number 21. No cattle guard. Instead, a powered gate of unpainted metal flashed past. About eight hundred meters behind the gate, two pole-mounted lights glowed. One over the front yard of a one-story rambler house clad in slabs of native limestone, the other over the closed carriage doors of a sheet metal barn.

Gravel rumbled under the tires. The razor wire fence passed monotonously by.

"The taxidermist should have had plenty of room in that barn to work," Portia said.

Dowling sucked air through his teeth. "We still haven't proven anything. Let's take a squizz at the sat imagery."

Portia's neury overlaid an aerial still image onto her view of the left-hand window. A summery patchwork of greens lay between a narrow beige strip and a zone of deeper, splotchier green. The deeper green meant cycads and ferns foresting the dino preserve. Shadows stretching from some of the green patches and splotches indicated groves of trees. Other shadows flowed from contours of the land. Two squared-off shadows marked the house and barn.

"Bugger. The image is too old. Taken before Martinson rented the farm. But it can still tell us some things." He swept his fingertip over a green patch and the edge of a shadowed zone. "This is the grove and the ridge we saw from the road." His fingertip circled the full zone of shadow and a sunlit area between the shadow and the dino preserve. "I wonder if you can see this area from the neighboring farms."

His finger tapped air. The image zoomed in on the fence near the front corner shared with the Yeardleys. With a smile in his voice, Dowling said, "You little ripper!"

"What do you see?"

"Check the fencepost shadows between the two farms."

After a moment, Portia's eyebrows lifted. "They're the same lengths."

"Which means?"

"Martinson had the tall razor wire fence built."

"Highly likely... but still not proof."

The ute approached the lane of the next farm. "Chuck a yewy here," Dowling told the vehicle. It slowed and made a three-point turn. A brief respite from the rattle of the ute along the gravel road.

"Back to Blenheim?" Portia asked.

The ute picked up speed. The augmented reality view of farmland to the right vanished in a blink.

Dowling tugged the camera off the window. "Not yet. We've seen all we can from the road. But I reckon the Yeardleys might let us take a squizz from another angle."

CHAPTER 4

The Yeardleys' house, a two-story bungalow of honey-colored bricks and an umber-red metal roof rippled to look like spanish tile, sat primly and properly at the crest of a gentle rise. A veranda running the full front of the house held rocking chairs, a loveseat on a porch swing, and a small wicker table. Small flowerbeds under shining growlights dotted the broad front lawn and ringed the bases of oaks with roses and lilies.

As a girl, Portia had played with fairy dolls in her mum's flowerbeds, much like these.... but the calligraphed signs jutting up from the mulched soil, quoting Bible verses with extra flourishes on the capital letters in *Lord* and *God*, suggested that fairy dolls had best land elsewhere.

Dowling led the way across the lawn on a concrete footpath. The scent of fresh-cut grass mingled with the earthiness of the flowerbeds. Oak branches reached for each other overhead, like the loving elderly couple transformed into trees in some myth from ancient ancient Greece.

Pagan myths might be unwelcome here, too.

Lights snapped on at the edge of the veranda's roof. The spring of a storm door twanged and Portia squinted at the front door of the house.

A matronly figure stepped onto the veranda. A loose-fitting dress covered her from neck to wrists and ankles. "G'day."

Dowling's footsteps scraped to a halt on the concrete. He looked up and inclined his head a few centimeters. "G'day. I'm Special Agent Dowling, Frontier Police." He flashed his badge, then gestured palm-up toward Portia. "This is Do—Miss Oakeshott."

Portia bowed. She put on a smile her grandmother would be proud of. "G'day. Mrs. Yeardley?"

"Yes." Mrs. Yeardley pivoted her gaze to Dowling. Portia couldn't place her lilting accent. "Frontier Police? Is something the matter?"

"Not here. Your farm is a lovely spread. Places like this make me excited to go to the office every morning."

Portia's vision adapted well enough to make out Mrs. Yeardley's demure smile. "We strive to always do what is pleasing in the sight of the Lord." The smile faded. "Something is the matter elsewhere?"

Dowling's face looked pained. He angled his head in the direction of Martinson's farm.

Mrs. Yeardley wrung her hands, then gestured at the rocking chairs and porch swing. "Come on up, have a seat. I'll ask my husband to join us. Would you care for tea? A caf? A soft drink?"

Portia and the special agent made their requests. Another twang of the storm door's spring. They waited on the veranda while the muffled voices and pounding footsteps of children drifted to them from inside the house. The floodlights aimed at the yard turned off, sending the veranda into a cool but comfortable semi-darkness lit only by lamps inside the house diffused by lace curtains across the windows.

Mrs. Yeardley emerged five minutes later with a steel tray bearing drinks. With her came a man with black hair receding from the sides of his forehead. He raised a thick arm bulging against the unwrinkled sleeve of a flannel shirt. "G'day, special agent, I'm Mick Yeardley," he said in a gravelly voice as he shook Dowling's hand. Portia couldn't place his accent, either.

"Please, sit," Mrs. Yeardley added.

Dowling took one of the rocking chairs, Portia the other. Mrs. Yeardley handed out drinks, then joined her husband on the porch swing. The warmth of Portia's steaming cuppa softened the cool of the evening. Giggles sounded from just the other side of the wall.

"The missus says you're here about our neighbor?" asked Yeardley.

"Yes. First, what can you tell us about him?"

"Well, we never see the bloke. He lives up Port Bounty most of the time but you prolly know that. We can tell he's in if the lights are on at the house or we see cars up and down the road."

"What times is he about?" Dowling asked.

"Winters. Three or four days at a stretch." THe storm door's spring squeaked. Without turning his head, Yeardley said, voice firm, "You lot need to go to bed. We have to get up at one o'clock to make it to church, remember?"

Portia shivered and pulled her tea cup closer to her body. Twenty-four-sevens. They'd be offended if you called them that. Church of Christ Risen on the First Day. Fanatics who kept their church calendar by Earth's, instead of the thirty-four-hour days and seven or eight day weeks of New New South Wales. Portia had heard of the denomination, but had never met an adherent growing up in Esperance Heights' leafy suburban streets.

"Children," Yeardley said, his voice honed to sharper edge.

Portia craned her neck. A boy of perhaps five standard and a girl a couple of standard years older, both with cheeky looks on their faces, darted back from the storm door, trailing giggles.

"Go on, you heard Dad," a teenaged boy called after them. His voice warbled. He peered out the open door. A gangly build, dark brown hair slicked against his scalp, acne splotching his face. Portia remembered awkward boys at school dances. His brown-eyed gaze met hers and grew puzzled. "Are you a fronto?"

Dowling leaned forward. "Yes."

Yeardley swiveled and fixed the boy with a gimlet eye. "It's not just the young ones who need to go to bed."

The boy's brown eyes turned down. "Yes, Dad."

Yeardley's mouth quirked. "They're good sprats, most of the time."

"We regret the inconvenience," said Dowling. "We didn't know they had an early bedtime today."

"No, no. I'm glad Martinson ended up on your radar."

Portia's head made a half-turn before she could think. Had a shadow crossed the curtained window behind her? She blinked and sipped tea. Maybe she was seeing things.

Yeardley showed no sign of noticing anything either. To his wife, he said, "Beloved, be a helpmeet and get the kids to bed."

"Gladly." Mrs. Yeardley stood up, set down her fizzing cola on the side table. Her husband took her arms and pulled her down for a kiss. She walked toward the front door with a pleased smile on her face.

After the screen door twanged behind her, Yeardley planted his foot and brought the porch swing to a stop. "I don't think she could add anything to what I can tell you, and I'd rather we not talk about it in front of her."

Dowling scooted forward. The back ends of his chair's rockers poked into the air like bony spikes on a *Kunbarrasaurus'* tail. "What can you tell us?"

"As we said, we can sometimes see cars heading up Martinson's lane. I was working the side paddock late one winter night, this was, two local years ago? Yeah, two. One of the heifers was about to drop her first calf and she wandered off and," Yeardley drew a breath, "a team of frontos don't need to hear about a farmer's troubles."

Dowling nodded. "You were in the side paddock?"

"Yeah, it was, oh bugger, two or three o'clock. I was on a gentle rise and could see the full thousand meters to Martinson's lane and house. A car rolls up and out come three, ah...." Yeardley avoided Portia's gaze.

"You can't offend me," she said, feeling a naughty thrill as she fibbed to the man. "I've worked vice."

Dowling coughed. He raised an eyebrow at her. The farmer wasn't watching her, so she winked back.

Yeardley thickly swallowed. In the dim light, Portia couldn't tell if her words made him blush. "Yes," he said, "three of them, and their attire and demeanor left no doubt how they came by their quid."

"I see," Dowling said. "Thank you. Our investigation had not yet turned up any evidence of, ah, white slavery."

"I'm glad I brought it to your attention, then. We're good people, not just those of who believe He rose on the first day, but almost everyone around here. We don't want that element getting a foothold."

"We understand," Portia said. She sneaked a glance at Dowling. Couldn't he get the farmer on point?

The special agent extended his hand toward her, palm down, and dribbled air like a basketball. All the while he kept his gaze on Yeardley. "We knew a girl disappeared but we didn't know she worked in that trade."

"Disappeared?"

"No one talks about the missing girl?"

"We don't talk about women of ill repute, whether live or dead." Yeardley raised an insulated metal cup of tea to his mouth, but didn't sip. "Though she is a child of God, no matter how far she wandered from the Good Shepherd's flock."

Dowling paused. "Do you know something?"

"From time to time we hear gunshots from Martinson's place. Enough to get dinos on the preserve bellowing like a bull trying to get to a cow in heat. We can't see where Martinson's shooting from or what he's shooting at, but it sounds like they come from his back paddock." Yeardley waved in the direction of the wooded slope on Martinson's farm. "Could he have...?"

"It's possible," Dowling said.

"And sometimes clanking sounds. I thought of earth-moving equipment. Dear God." From the sound of Yeardley's voice, Portia guessed his face had drained of blood.

Dowling said, "I know you're a good family man and you have to wake up at one o'clock for church the same as your wife and children. Would you grant us permission to recon his farm from your side paddock? When we're done, we'll drive off without needing to bother you."

"What do you think you can find?"

"We don't know. We want to gather as much evidence as we can to maximize the chance the judge approves the search warrant."

Yeardley huffed out a breath. "Search warrants. The Americans collapsed because they rejected God, and we emulate their ways."

"I hear you," Dowling said. Amazing how his tone of voice could imply agreement when his words were noncommital. "But officially, we're limited to saying, make those wishes known to your MP."

Yeardley nodded. "The side paddocks are fallow. We keep the cattle close to the hay barn during the dark weeks. God bless you both."

All rose and shook hands. Dowling led the way off the veranda and across dormant grass. They rounded the corner of the house and into a cool breeze from the south. He walked through a rectangle of light thrown onto the lawn from an upstairs window. A line crossed the rectangle near the house and the light slowly rippled. Portia glanced up. A window open a crack. Throw on a blankey for good sleeping weather.

"What do you think we'll see?" she asked.

The special agent grunted. His feet left soft grass for the crunch of the gravel lane.

The lane ended at a sheet metal barn with a pitched roof. The smell of hay lightly touched Portia's nose. Behind the barn, a cattlebeast mooed in sleepy contentment.

Light from the house dimmed with distance. A glance back showed Portia the upstairs window had gone dark. Gloom shrouded the ground and turned the barn ghostly gray. She glanced up at the stars. That red dot was Stella Australis B, the lesser star in their binary system. She remembered as a child marveling at stories and pictures of the moon of far-off Earth.

Dowling pulled a flashlight from his inner pocket. He hooked a curled piece around his ear and turned on the light. When he glanced down, a pallid circle a meter across lit up the ground. Enough illumination to see a hole before one twisted an ankle in it.

They came to a slatted metal gate one-meter-fifty high and wide enough for a ute. Dowling glanced at the chain binding it to a post, then at Portia. "You up for a climb?" He didn't wait for a reply. Instead he went up the slats like a ladder, swung his legs over the top, and jumped backward to the ground on the far side.

Her arms moved freely in her jacket. Dowling led her feet with the light as she did the same.

They were in a paddock, yet with fences so small and distant she imagined walking across an open prairie. Tufted grass swatted at her shins. Crickets jumped whizzing along the ground. The special agent veered his path around crumbly brown chips of dried cow manure.

Portia trudged on. The image of the winner cow's mounted head came to the inside of her eyelids when she blinked. What evidence might they find that would do right by her?

"If Yeardley didn't see anything from his side paddock," she said, "what makes you think you will?"

"We don't have to *see* anything, doctor," said Dowling over his shoulder. He stopped walking. "Come to think of it, here's as good a place to calibrate the sniffer as any." He reached into his jacket.

"How many pockets do you have in your jacket?"

"Enough." His voice revealed he grinned. He brought out an object and glanced down to his hand. The flashlight over his ear bathed the object in light.

A gray plastic cube, tiny against his palm, with a funnel as long as the cube's main body jutting from a side. A molded plastic ring flanged off the opposite side. He tapped a button on another side, or was the entire side the button? A fan whined at high speed. LEDs cycled yellow, then green.

He clipped the molded plastic ring to a carabiner on his jacket. "I'll share you the baseline," the special agent said.

Portia's neury popped text over her vision where the dark, rolling field met the star-crusted sky.

Cadaverine < 1 ppm

Putrescine < 1 ppm

Geosmin < 5 ppm

and other compounds she didn't immediately recognize. She didn't need to. Her nose wrinkled at a memory of the first two compounds in a training lab. Unmistakable indicators of rotting flesh. The third compound was the scent of freshly-dug earth.

Which meant... "You think Martinson buried the dinos near the preserve's perimeter?"

The cool breeze rustled the leaves of a dozen sweetgum trees. "There's a chance they're buried on the farm. That gives him a defense that they wandered off the preserve and were fair game."

A hundred meters farther, a trickle came to her ears. A jagged gash across the ground twenty meters ahead had to be a gully with flowing water. Dowling's flashlight panned across a patch of bare dirt gouging out the gully wall. Cattle hooves had cratered the patch. Portia waved her arms for balance and the special agent aimed his beam at the ground in front of her.

After they hopped the trickling watercourse and scrambled up the gully's far bank, Portia said, "That can't be it. Mr. Pietrangelo said surveillance video showed no dinos crossed the perimeter—what?"

Dowling grabbed her forearm. He peered into the gloom, in the direction of the sweetgums. In a harsh whisper, he asked, "You hear anything?"

Portia angled her head and cupped her hand behind her ear. "No," she murmured.

"All those days and weeks crossing the system in tin cans, I lost some hearing. Let's keep moving." He led her across the field, in the direction of the wooded ridge hiding Martinson's back paddock from sight.

She checked the numbers from the special agent's sniffer.

Cadaverine 2 ppm

Putrescine 3 ppm

Geosmin 7 ppm

Random fluctuations? Plenty of things died on a farm, and a wild animal digging a burrow could kick up some fresh earth.

"Back to what you were saying," the special agent said. "I hate to have to tell you, but regardless where he shot the dinos or buried them, Martinson had help from an employee of your company."

Portia vigorously shook her head, certain he could hear her gesture in the gloom. "He could have stolen the keys to earth-moving equipment. Especially if he's active in winter."

"Or he hired someone in company security to lose the audio and video of him herding a dino across the perimeter."

They came to a barbed-wire fence separating two paddocks of the Yeardleys' farm. While Dowling clambered easily over, she rolled her lips together. Company employees helping the poacher? Her stomach soured. "Good Lord, I hope you're wrong."

He shone the flashlight on the fence and gave her a hand. Enough space separated the barbs for her to put hands and feet on the strands. She pulled her arms in but still her jacket snagged on the top wire. Dowling helped her work the jacket loose with one hand while his other held her forearm. The taut wires wobbled like a high-wire act at a circus. She reached the ground without shredding her jacket.

Country life was not for her.

They continued across the paddock. Her neury's compass showed they headed southeast. The terrain rolled but generally fell to a grove of trees looming ahead in the starlight. Branches rustled in the breeze. An owl hooted and some small creature darted into undergrowth as Portia and the special agent entered the grove.

Dowling's hand rasped over a trunk. "Oaks."

She remembered gnarled branches swooping low enough to her back lawn for her seven-year-old self to sit on one while her bare toes brushed the ground. Here amid these oaks, the air seemed a trifle warmer and the musty smell of fallen leaves came pleasantly to her nose.

Something metallic glimmered between trees a dozen meters away. Portia gave a double-take, then let out a breath. One of the tall fence-posts of Martinson's farm.

Dowling wound his way through the trees. He stopped next to the fencepost and slapped his hand onto it. It rang faintly, unnatural in the winter night.

Cadaverine 5 ppm

Putrescine 8 ppm

Geosmin 17 ppm

Dowling looked past the fencepost. Barbed wire gleamed in the flashlight glow. Barbs sharper and more hooked than the ones between the Yeardleys' paddocks. Somewhere behind her, another small creature ran through the brush as if it too fled this monstrous fence. She hugged her arms against her torso.

The flashlight swept on, toward the ridgeline hiding Martinson's back paddock. The dark ground and immense vault of sky swallowed the flashlight beam.

What else had the ground swallowed?

The special agent's voice broke the night with a tone of pleased righteousness. "The decay and earth-moving molecules getting more prevalent the closer we get to the farm, plus Yeardley's statement about gunshots, bellowing dinos, and earth-moving equipment, add that to the grotesqueries in Martinson's basement in Port Bounty, and the judge will sign off on a warrant."

A fallen twig snapped three or four meters behind them. A young male voice warbled, "No he won't."

CHAPTER 5

ortia's head snapped around. Next to an oak about four meters away, the beam of Dowling's flashlight threw a weak glow on the Yeardleys' teenage son.

And the rifle he held diagonally across his chest.

"Hands where I can see them," the boy said.

Dowling slowly spread his arms. He spoke slowly, casually, "What's all this about, mate?"

How? Portia's legs felt immobile, like concrete pillars sunk into the earth. Yet she wanted to run. Fast as she could.

The boy shifted his hands. Light danced along the rifle's front sight and the end of the barrel. The muzzle was the jet-black iris of a one-eyed carrion god.

With more warble in his voice, the boy said, "You know too much."

"Mate. Don't be the devil's own fool. I'm a fronto. My neury sends my location to headquarters round the clock. Even way out here at the bottom of the world. If something happens to Dr. Oakeshott or me, a paramilitary team will descend on our last known location. You'd be punished to the fullest extent of the law."

The boy angled the rifle's muzzle closer to Portia and the special agent. His eyes looked lifeless inside the grim mask of his face.

Portia's cheeks turned clammy as a corpse's. All Dowling had were words. The boy had a rifle and she couldn't move her legs to run and if she did the boy'd put a bullet through her back or blow a hole in her skull.

"And," Dowling said, "you'd break your Mum's heart."

The boy's face turned slack. His chest heaved with a breath. He pivoted the rifle, butt toward the ground, muzzle toward the underside of his chin—

"Bloody hell!" Dowling sprinted like a footy tagger out to tackle a ball carrier. But instead of wrapping his arms around the boy, he grabbed the rifle barrel at a full passing run and yanked the teenager off-balance.

The rifle roared in the night. The special agent and the boy tumbled amid the roots of oaks as birds squawked and beat their wings.

Portia unfroze in an instant. Ears ringing, she ran forward, aiming for the wobbling circle of illumination from Dowling's flashlight. The special agent flung the rifle away. It clattered into the darkness.

She kneeled beside Dowling. "Are you hurt?"

"What?" He squinted and massaged his ear with one hand. The look on his face showed he only guessed at her words. "I'm tinny."

Unhurt. Thank God. And the boy? He lay on the ground, his dark brown hair an unruly mess. He breathed rapidly and his eyes were squeezed shut.

Shock? She checked his pulse with fingertips at his neck while counting breaths. No sight nor smell of blood.

Also unhurt. Thank God for that, too.

The boy's hand fluttered up to his neck. His fingers clamped on her hand. His whole arm shook. "Almighty God what I have I done Almighty God."

"There there." Portia could think of nothing more to say.

"Oh God Almighty God I've already broken her heart."

If you were a mother? If he were your boy? "No. She'll forgive you. He who Rose on the First Day will forgive you. But you've got to tell us everything they'll forgive you for."

Dowling gave her a grin, like a geiersaur preparing to wolf down fresh kill. She raised her eyebrows and hardened her jaw. A moment later he lowered his abashed gaze to the boy's face.

The boy's arm stilled. His crushing grip on Portia's hand eased. "I will."

"Can you sit up?"

He nodded and let go of her hand. With a wince, he pushed himself up on his elbows, then scooted on his rump to put his back against the nearest oak. His breaths slowed. He avoided their eyes.

"When Martinson rented the place, he needed workers to put up the new fence. Local boys. Dad said good on ya, sweat like a man in the summer sun and earn some money, just as long as you keep Sunday as the Sabbath. I was nervous as can be. Fourteen standard, and Martinson was this laired-up rich bloke all the way from *Port Bounty*. But instead of mocking me as a twenty-four-sevener, he brought me in on the joke. We'd be mates and tell Dad and Mum what they wanted to hear." He thumped the back of his head against the tree trunk. "Mum."

Dowling opened his mouth. Portia extended her hand to him and spoke instead. "Tell us more about Martinson, if you would."

"So we're building the fence and I work up the nerve to ask why it's so bloody high. Why the razor wire on top angles in. Why he built a gate at the back boundary with the dinosaur preserve."

Dowling and Portia looked at each other.

The boy went on. "He winked and said he couldn't tell a boy, but he could tell a man." He squeezed shut his eyes. Mucus clogged his warbly voice. "I took the things he offered. I played with playing cards. I drank intoxicating liquor. I fornicated with harlots."

"And then he told you...?"

"He wanted to hunt dinosaurs. Before, he'd done it the right way, paying a fee for a permit. But if the dinos went walkabout off the preserve, he could bag them for free. And if I helped them go walkabout, he'd pay me a dinkum wage. I told myself every Sunday I'd tithe every quid he paid me. Almighty God, I was a fool. You can launder money but you can't launder sin."

"He put you in a tough spot," Portia said. A shard of anger spiked up her spine, carrying the winner cow's mounted head like an *hors d'oeuvre* on a skewer. She exhaled and kept her voice sympathetic. "How did you help them go walkabout?"

"There were four of us." He named the other three.

"They live around here?" Dowling asked. "About your age?"

"Between here and Blenheim. I was the youngest," the boy said, then shook his head as if that were no excuse. "He'd have us turn off our neurys and communicate with each other and him encrypted through short-range radio. We'd open the perimeter gate and enter the preserve on foot. We'd track them. Wasn't hard. They're active all winter and they don't expect hunters those weeks. A lot of the females are sitting their nests."

The boy swallowed. "We'd herd them through the perimeter gate to the back paddock. The four-legged ones with armored plates, minmis and kunbarrasaurs, were easy. Stupid and timid. The flightless bird-like ones too. We lured the stralla with a side of a riddlepig dead of natural causes. Towed the dead pig behind a one-man four-wheeler."

His voice cracked like a thin eggshell. "Only the winner was a challenge. Put me in awe that Almighty God once made something so bonzer. She moved quickly for something so huge. One of me mates almost got his foot stomped."

Portia spoke. "What about the cameras and microphones at the preserve's perimeter?"

"I asked Martinson about it. He laughed it off. Said he had a bloke inside company security in Blenheim who'd scrub the data."

She shivered inside her jacket. "What was the bloke's name?"

"Martinson didn't say."

Did he need to? Someone like the special agent could interrogate everyone working in security in Blenheim and unearth the turncoat.

And speaking of *unearth*... a chill flowed through her gut, but she didn't shiver. Instead she felt numb. "What happened at the back paddock?"

"We shut the gate and herded them toward the woods on the back slope." For three slow breaths he looked that direction in the darkness. "Martinson waited in a blind. We cleared out from downrange and he fired. Easy peasy," he added. Shame flooded his voice.

"Did he have you do more?"

"We'd skin them, butcher them, and measure them for taxidermy right where he felled them. The skins went off to the barn. He flew a bloke in all the way from Cookland."

Dowling rubbed against the grain of his beard stubble. "Martinson didn't say this bloke's name, either."

"That'd be right. I remember some of how he looked. A couple centimeters shorter than you. Nose long and narrow and tipped up at the end like a waterslide. He had all the equipment in the barn to make the mannequins and mount the skins. The meat, we'd carve off hunks and cook them over a firepit. The winner's ribeye, medium rare, it melted in my mouth...."

His lips and jaw worked. Portia guessed the boy's mouth watered. Then his torso convulsed in waves. He leaned away from them and retched. Foul sounds, a bilious stench. Her nose wrinkled and she had to look away.

"There's another question I have to ask," said the special agent. "What did you do with the rest of the dino carcasses?"

The boy spoke in a monotone, as if only fumes remained in his emotional fuel tank. "We had earth-moving equipment. Just like Dad talked about on the veranda with you. The bedroom window was cracked wide enough I could hear every word."

"We gathered that," Dowling said.

A breeze skittered through the oak branches above. Portia shivered again. She hadn't even thought about how the boy had learned they investigated Martinson.

"The earth movers scraped out pits," the teenager said, "shoved the carcasses in, then scraped the dirt back over. I didn't control the machinery. I helped tamp down the dirt and lay sod on top. And rig up grow lights to make sure the sod would take by summer."

Dowling turned to Portia. A quick dip of her chin confirmed what she'd guessed. The boy's testimony, along with their other evidence, would give them a warrant to search Martinson's farm. To uncover the skeletons and rotting flesh of dinos killed for a rich young man's vanity. Even if the dead dinos were only a wedge to punish Martinson for a more heinous crime, he would be punished, and their bones could lie more restfully under the impartial scales of justice.

The boy shifted against the tree trunk. He regarded Portia and Dowling. The wan light from the flashlight lit up a flicker of hope, but then his pimpled face slumped and his shoulders fell. "What comes next?"

"Your mum and the good Lord might forgive you," Dickinson said, "but you still violated Dinosaur Hunting Act 2749. I've got to tell your parents and then take you in for that."

The boy bowed his head. "I sinned. I have to pay the price for it."

Overhead, the rustle of branches eased. The air lay still in the grove. Yet still Portia shivered, more violently than before, like a dishrag getting poison wrung out. "An-an-and you threatened a fronto with a deadly weapon!"

Dowling laid his palm on Portia's forearm. He gave the boy a firm but clement look. "The ref can keep the whistle in his pocket and call advantage on that one, I think."

Portia dropped from her knee. Her rump landed on the cold ground. She hugged herself and leaned toward Dowling. Thank God the special agent knew what to do.

"Can you walk, mate?" he asked the boy.

A nod. The boy staggered to his feet. He steadied himself with one hand on the oak's ribbed trunk.

Dowling picked up the rifle and slung it over his shoulder. "Go first."

Another nod. The boy trudged, gaze cast down on the ground, through the grove of oaks. They soon came to open paddock. A thousand meters away, the few lights of the Yeardleys' farmhouse faintly glowed, outshone by the glittering sprawl of the south polar stars. In the distance, kilometers behind Portia, sounded the protective bellow of a winner bull.

MINNIE AND THE TREKKER

MINNIE AND THE TREKKER

Behind the stalk of a fern as tall as a man, Portia Oakeshott stretched prone on the soft ground of the cycad forest. The thick smell of fecund soil filled her nose. A small stream trickled nearby. Mosquitoes buzzed around her ears despite sprayed-on repellent and her waving hands. Stella Australis A, hanging low in the sky to her left, to the north, filled the forest with slanted shafts of red-orange light, like the stained-glass windows of a church filled with funerary lilies.

Even when he whispered, the voice of McAdams, the field ecologist, carried over the sounds of chirping fliers and rustling foliage. "There she is, where that adventure trekker said she was, down to the meter." He aimed his chin toward a brown, rounded shape looming over the fallen bole of a palm-like cycad. The shape looked like a boulder.

"Take a squizz." McAdams handed Portia the binoculars.

Propped on her elbows, she moved the binoculars to her eyes. Servos hummed as the lenses adjusted focus past the fern's drooping fronds and onto the rounded shape a hundred meters away.

No doubt it was a minnie. A female *Minmi paravertebra novacambrianovaaustraliensis*, a four-legged herbivore that off-world tourists said looked like a midget stegosaurus that lost its sail-like armor plates. When Portia heard that, she gritted her teeth and gave a polite smile to make her grandmother proud.

Lines of bony protrusions studded the minnie's back from neck to tail. More protrusions, smaller and spikier, surrounded her face like an elizabeth collar. The soft jaw and nasal ridge tapered to a snout as dainty as one could imagine on a creature three meters from nose to tail and weighing a third of a ton.

But her face—

"My God, she looks in horrid shape." A mouth cracked and dry. Sunken cheeks. Sunken eyes, too, blinking slowly against a troop of blue-black flies buzzing and swarming over her.

Portia's blood ran cold. The last thing a dinosaur veterinarian wanted to see. Was the minnie dead?

The dino stirred her head. The flies scattered. Relief washed through Portia. But only for a moment. The dino lay its head against the cycad's trunk and its eyelids slid shut. One by one, flies returned to its face.

Portia scanned with the binoculars. The minnie's shriveled flanks rose and fell with quick and shallow breaths. She hid her belly behind her four legs, each bent on splayed knees. Her legs formed walls, her body a roof—

"She's sitting on a clutch of eggs."

McAdams lifted his digger hat with its buttoned-up side brim. His other hand brushed graying, wavy hair back from his forehead. "Too right. The only question is, which is sick? The minnie or her eggs?"

"Only one way to find out." Portia shrugged their tranquilizer gun off her shoulder. She held it out to him.

"You don't want to take the shot?"

"I've taken it to the range at headquarters, but I'm not as good a shot as you."

He took the trank gun. She twisted onto her side. Something woody jabbed her in the ribs. She lifted the flap of her hip pack. A line of trank darts with a rainbow of colored bands showing weight ranges. She pulled out the dart ringed with yellow and held it in front of her eyes.

"What do you make her weight? Three hundred kilos?"

His bulging eyes peered at the minnie. "More like two-fifty," McAdams said.

Too much sedative might slow the minnie's brainstem enough to stop her heart. They could always increase the dosage if they had to. Portia squirted a quarter of the dart's volume onto the ground. She handed over the dart, then focused on using the instep of her right boot to scratch at something biting her left leg just above the ankle.

Pang zip. She looked up.

The minnie's head lifted from its resting place against the fallen cycad and turned toward her flank. The yellow-banded trank dart bobbed against the sliver of belly exposed between a line of bony protrusions down her back and her thick, folded legs. Then the minnie's head drooped and her eyes gently shut.

Portia and McAdams stood. He held out the trank gun. His real rifle, one with the caliber and muzzle velocity to take down a six-meter *Australovenator*, clanked against his shoulder.

She brushed dirt, bits of leaf, and crawling insects off her multi-pocketed shirt and cargo pants, then took the trank gun. She slung it over her shoulder and walked half a step behind him through patchy undergrowth. Mosses as slippery as banana peels covered flat rocks. Gnarled mushrooms smeared umber and ochre stains along the sides of her boots.

The minnie smelled like the chimera built up from lizard, elephant, and ostrich genes that it was. As pleasant as a zoo on a cool spring day. The minnie's flanks rose and fell with the tempo of slow pastoral music. A raspy gargle sounded in each breath. Still, her unconscious face looked almost peaceful.

What had driven her to this state? Less than a day, roughly thirty hours, since the adventure trekker, backpacking alone through the dinosaur preserve after paying hefty fees to both the company and his insurance carrier, called the company's field office in Tallis. Though taken at a range of eighty meters, his photos and video matched what Portia saw.

As Portia and McAdams drew closer, other odors crawled into her nose. Sulfur and rot. She wrinkled her nose and ignored the odors as best she could. First, attend your patient.

She pulled a scanner from her medical kit. She touched the minnie's back between bony protrusions. Skin like boiled leather. The minnie didn't flinch.

"You got the right dose," McAdams said. His voice boomed, but the minnie remained motionless.

Portia aimed the scanner's infrared and acoustic ports at the proper spots on the minnie's neck and belly. Her neuronal interface projected the results onto her optic nerves as a translucent panel floating above the dino's back. Heart and respiration rates slow, but not acutely dangerous. Body temperature normal enough.

Another item from her medical kit, a blood analyzer. She pressed the extractor patch against the minnie's side with her palm. A green light blinked on the patch. She stepped back, wadded up the patch around its central bump of hardware, and wedged the patch into the base unit.

More data popped into her vision. Blood sugar low. Ketones high. She could look at the rest later. Right now, it only mattered that the starving minnie's body had started digesting itself.

Not moving even for food or water for days at a time… only one thing could compel a female of any species to that extreme. "How do we take a look at her eggs?"

"I'll have a go." McAdams unslung his rifle from his shoulder. Portia's breath caught until he wedged the rifle's stock between the minnie's rear foot and her flank. He grunted and groaned. After thirty seconds of prying, he pulled the minnie's rear foot far enough for Portia to see the eggs the dino sheltered.

And for the stench of decay to billow out.

Portia gagged. Her long fingers pinched shut her nostrils. "Strewth, are they all dead?"

McAdams lay flat and peered underneath the minnie. He squinted, then reached for a flashlight from one of the pockets of his cargo pants. Though the flashlight was the size of his little finger, one click of its button threw sharp-edged whiteness into the hollow between the dino's belly and the ground.

"I'll loan you a squizz through my eyes," he said.

"Sure." Portia stepped back a meter from the minnie and turned for fresher air. She inhaled deeply without gagging. Recentered, with a thought she opened the video feed from McAdams' optic nerves.

Five leathery eggs, each the size and oblong oval shape of a football, each one half-buried in the soil. Each one broken. The top of each egg littered the ground. Horizontal gouges and dangling slivers of casing showed something had repeatedly slashed across each egg. Columns of bulldog ants, so large they seemed a perfect match for the dinosaur preserve even though they still existed on Earth, marched up and down the eggs porting bits of the outer casing back to their hives.

The light jumped and the view angled—McAdams moved his head for a better view.

The eggs looked empty. Whatever new life once held inside had been ripped out.

McAdams sighed and cut the feed. He leaned back and rubbed his forehead under the brim of his hat. "Crikey, those eggs came the raw prawn."

Portia came closer to the minnie and squatted near the dinosaur's dormant head. The stink from the broken eggs no longer triggered her disgust. With a wave of melancholy in her voice, she said, "The minnie left her eggs for a few minutes for water or some tucker. While she was away, a predator came along and ate them." She patted the dino's skin between bony protrusions on her back. Poor girl. "But why is she still incubating them? Her brain might be small for her body, but it must know her eggs are dead."

"She's getting along in years." McAdams extended his fingers toward the minnie's face. The wrinkles and puffy skin evidencing her age became apparent. Portia pulled apart the minnie's lips. Tartar stained the sides of worn molars. A hairline crack ran down one of her back teeth.

"I see that, but what does her being old have to do with her incubating dead eggs?"

McAdams gave a wry smile. "You're too young."

Portia raised her chin. "I'm twenty-four standard. This is my eleventh local year with the company." Granted, the local year on New

New South Wales lasted a little over six weeks of thirty-four hour days, but she wasn't a rookie anymore.

"Still too young to hear the tick of the proverbial biological clock. This might have been the last set of eggs our minnie can lay. Maybe she lost more than the usual amount of young from her earlier matings. So she got clucky and is obsessing over them to the point of dying of thirst."

Portia straightened her back. "There's more to the female mind than obsessing over reproductive partners and offspring."

"Yeah." McAdams lifted his hat and scratched in his graying hair. "But if there were less, none of us would be here."

Portia turned her gaze to the minnie's sunken face. "I'll give her intravenous fluids and slip in a mood stabilizer."

"Worth doing," McAdams said. "I'll work on a report."

A breeze rustled the fronds of the cycads. Portia brushed a mosquito away from her face, then reached into her medical kit.

A transparent bag of white powders. A water distiller with a built-in ultraviolet sterilizer. She pulled out the distiller's funnel. "We need water."

McAdams pulled the stopper from his canteen and poured in a liter. The distiller chugged for a time. A blinking yellow light indicated a sterilizer cycle, changing to solid green when it completed.

With deft fingers, Portia connected the powder bag to the sterile water outlet port. While water gurgled in and the powder dissolved, she tore open the packaging of an injection assembly and mounted it on the other end of the pack.

From the distance came a dinosaur's long, bass bellow. A second interrupted the first. Tinos, both of them: *Diamantinasaurus* bulls. Probably a bachelor male challenging an old bull for ownership of the old bull's harem.

The male mind also obsessed over reproductive partners and offspring, didn't it?

She refocused on her work. The injection assembly had a side port. There she mounted a yellow-tinged solution of mood stabilizer. A controlled substance—her neury alerted her that it would report the mood stabilizer's use to the Royal Pharmacological Monitoring Board.

Fine. This wasn't an urban woman in need of a hobby. The preserve's dinosaurs were expensive combinations of fossil reconstructions, spliced DNA, educated guesswork, and Aussie pride. The preserve attracted tourists from the big cities of Cookland, the northern continent, and a growing number from off-world. The more dinosaurs alive on the preserve, the better for the tourist trade. And if by chance McAdams overestimated her age, and the minnie laid another clutch of eggs....

Her eyes bright with hope, Portia worked on the leg previously pried straight by McAdams. After long seconds hunting the dehydrated minnie's vein, she found one. She brought the injection assembly close and it inserted its needle. The assembly's green lights blinked and its pump kicked in. Portia taped the needle and the bag in place against the minnie's rough skin.

Work complete, she stood and stretched her shoulders. A glance down showed the i.v. bag begin to shrink. "Ten minutes should do it."

"I've got the report almost written up," said McAdams. "But there's one open question. What got into her eggs?"

Despite the shafts of sunlight angling through the cycad forest, Portia shivered. "Did she accidentally crush them?" It happened from time to time. What emotions would a dinosaur feel, knowing she'd killed her own clutch of eggs? Enough to make her hysterically incubate them?

"Can't be. The tops would be resting on top and the breaks would be jagged if they'd been crushed from above, by her body or a falling object."

"Other dinosaurs?"

"Not a strallo." McAdams used the colloquial name for *Australovenator*. Not as big as the *T. rex* that off-worlders complained wasn't on the preserve, but still a six-meter long therapod, apex predator of Cretaceous Australia.

"Why not?"

"Couple reasons. A fair percentage of protein, but too small to be worth the candle. Same reason we don't eat insects. Also, see how close together the gouges and the dangling shreds are? A strallo's claw would rip through all that."

Portia nodded. "Speaking of insects, grackelsaurs have mouthparts adapted for eating them, so we can rule them out." She thought of other small, bird-like therapods. "Geiersaurs? They aren't obligate carrion eaters. They can eat live meat."

"Yeah, can."

She raised an eyebrow. "You're saying a modern mammal did this."

"Looks like cat claws, if I had to guess." He pawed at the air like a cat playing with a ball. Or a dying mouse.

Portia rubbed the side of her nose. "Does it? We're six klicks into the preserve. The only meat-eating modern mammals anywhere hereabout are cats and dogs on farms on the other side of the perimeter." The company well knew the threat carnivorous mammals posed to dino eggs. The gene techs gave strallos and other predators an instinct to hunt down by smell any dogs and cats that wandered into the preserve.

"The carnisaurs might have missed one." McAdams rolled his wrists to emphasize a shrug. "Rather than us argue, we can gather some evidence."

Without another word, he dropped to his belly and stuck one arm and his head into the crevice between the minnie's legs. He coughed. The dino's bulk muffled his next words. "Bugger, what a stink. Come on, you. Work loose.... got ya!"

McAdams scrambled away from the minnie and held up his prize. He turned his head away from the stench of rot. "Got a bag for this?"

Her long fingers already pulled one from a crevice of her medical kit. She pulled wide the open zip closure and held the bag at arm's length. He shoved in the broken egg and sealed it up.

The i.v. bag lay shriveled against the minnie's leg. One liter wouldn't save her life, but it gave her a chance to get to water. "Time to take out the i.v."

"No hurry. We have to watch till the trank wears off, right?"

A nod, then Portia squatted. She pulled tape and tossed the i.v. bag into the reinforced biohazard pocket of her kit. A quick dab of coagulant on the puncture site, then a biodegradable spray bandage that would slough off in a few days. When the cold aerosol touched her skin, the minnie's leg flinched.

The dino's eyes remained closed. Still. "Won't be long." Portia stood and ran through the mental checklist. She'd done all she could. "Back to our hiding spot."

A minute later, they lay behind the brushy fern. Portia looked through the binoculars. *Come on, girl, rise and shine.*

The minnie's head stirred. Her eyes opened. Though still full of sadness, they looked more alert than before. The dino's cheeks looked a tiny bit fuller, too. She raised her snout and sniffed.

Her legs unfolded. She clambered up, all wobbly. Her head drooped. Her gaze settled on the four broken eggs remaining half-buried in the ground.

Portia's breath caught.

After a long moment, the minnie turned and plodded toward the trickling stream.

———

The field office in Tallis was a small affair, concrete-block buildings three stories tall, laid out in a line between the two-lane road and the landing pad. Their quadrotor descended. Landing feet touched asphalt. Even before the quaddy's rotors stopped, Portia unbuckled. She hurried across the long shadows of the buildings with the broken egg tucked against her ribs with both hands.

Middle building, upper story, down the central corridor to the third room on the left. The sequencing lab. Scents of chemicals and air conditioning. The rounded plastic housing of the DNA sequencer on the back wall. The windows gave a view over houses and a cricket oval to the north. Stella Australis A dipped toward the horizon, silhouetting a church steeple and the local shire's offices.

With a mix of pop songs playing in her auditory nerves, she put on gloves and a face shield. A press of a button sterilized a work bench with ultraviolet light. She opened the bag and set the broken egg on the bench. With tools and test tubes processed in the autoclave, she set to work.

Swabs of amniotic fluid, in which might be mingled the saliva of a dog or a cat. She put the first one in the sequencer's amplification hopper and added in all the species-specific primers she could think of. Strallo, grackelsaur, geiersaur, ant, dog, cat, and human. While the amplifier chugged and whirred, with a scalpel she sliced off curlicues from the egg's slashed edge. They went into test tubes while she looked up how to extract DNA from them. Lyse the cells, then incubate with—

The sequencer dinged. Amplification—the process of subjecting DNA strands matching the primers to multiple rounds of doubling—complete. The sequencer now had enough copies of DNA from all the species for which she'd added primers to find out which one had ripped open the minnie's eggs. Sequencing proper would start now. Soon she'd know whether the cat was a Siamese or a Persian, the dog a Labrador or an Alsatian.

After extracting DNA from the egg cuttings, she stored those samples in the refrigerator, then looked up in surprise. Night had fallen, leaving only a rich twilight and the reflection of auto-on ceiling lights in the window.

She rolled her neck. How late had it gotten?

The sequencer played a cheerful ditty. Portia spun around. After the machine's display panel told her it had uploaded the sequence results to the company's servers at headquarters in Port Bounty, she launched the hopper's cleaning cycle. Through her neury, she told the sequencer, [Show me the sequence results.]

Lines of text popped into her vision. The words floated on the off-white wall above the sequencer.

Portia scanned down the list. And frowned.

Australovenator… Negative

Grackelsaurus… Negative

Geiersaurus… Negative

Canis familiaris… Negative

Felis familiaris… Negative…

Negative for every animal big enough to rip open a minnie egg. The only positives gave no clue. Some ant DNA, which fit with the insects she and McAdams had seen scavenging. Human DNA identified, after a search of the company's database, as belonging to Ridley McAdams, field ecologist.

A knock on the door. She'd left it open out of habit. Bulging eyes and wavy, salt-and-pepper hair. McAdams' voice boomed over the catchy trickle of pop music in her hearing. "Found me that cat yet?"

[Music off.] "No cat. Nor dog."

"What? Bugger. I have the report all drafted, except for identifying what got into the minnie's eggs." He brushed his fingers through his hair, then covered a yawn. "Maybe DNA on that first sample degraded too much in the field for the primers to amplify it. You can sequence more tomorrow. Let's catch a rideshare back to the flophouse."

Portia shook her head. "I'll run one more tonight." She had no qualms about spending time with McAdams after hours—a married man, he had daughters not much younger than her back in Port Bounty. The urge to solve the puzzle burned too strongly.

"See you in the morning, then," McAdams said.

Alone in the building, she returned to work. Into the sequencer went the next swab. In addition to the same panel as the first sequencing run, she added primers for a dozen more species that came to mind, from small carnivorous dinosaurs to large contemporary spiders to modern birds of prey. *Something* had to hit. Didn't it?

The amplifier chugged away for a time. With no work to do, Portia went down the hall to a sitting area with a small esky. She stepped up to the esky, planning to get a cup of tea.

Caffeinated? No, too late in the evening. [Decaf,] she told the machine. [Milk and one teaspoon sugar.] The esky's front panel display showed her order. An animated icon paired with the word *steeping*. Thirty seconds before it finished her cup. Time to file a maintenance request.

She lounged in a plush red armchair with squared-off cushions and sipped her cuppa. She restarted the music feed to her auditory nerves and wondered what to do.

From her flesh & blood memory came a memo from Pietrangelo, the company's operations director. *Involve yourselves with our neighbors near the preserve perimeter. There're only two types: those who like the company, and those who don't like the company yet.*

Portia nodded to herself. She surfed local webforums and news sites. Typical small town matters: a local boy had signed with the junior team of a cricket club in Endeavour Bay, the biggest city on Cookland, the more settled of the two continents. A shop in the town's high street, selling custom accessories for pets ranging from frogs and ferrets to fish, celebrated its first anniversary. The shire council table a debate about which minor farm road should next be paved with living asphalt. Her head lolled, and her eyelids with it.

A *ping* in her head roused her. The sequencer had amplified and sequenced the DNA. She gulped the last of her tea, put the cup and saucer in the hopper of the esky's dishwasher, and hurried back to the lab and the sequencer's output summary.

Australovenator… Negative

Grackelsaurus… Negative

Geiersaurus… Negative

Canis familiaris… Negative

Felis familiaris… Negative

Nothing new so far.

…Ozraptor… Negative

Hmm. So much for carnivorous dinosaurs. Had she forgotten any? No.

Selenocosmia crassipes… Negative

The whistling tarantula, like the bulldog ant, was descended from living stock brought from Earth. Perhaps just an urban legend that it could eat birds, let alone fetal dinosaurs.

Aquila audax… Negative….

The wedge-tailed eagle was the largest bird of prey on New New South Wales. And Portia's last chance of solving the mystery that night.

Portia returned to the field office the next morning a few minutes before thirteen. The self-driving rideshare let her out into bright sunlight for the walk into the laboratory building. The daylight boosted her mood. Taking the stairs up to the third floor got her blood flowing.

She didn't have an answer yet, but she held her chin up with the expectation she'd find one.

A flash of squared-off red, a hiss of hot water in the esky, bulging eyes and wavy hair. She paused at the sitting area. "G'day," she said to McAdams.

"Find anything last night?"

"No."

"That'd be right," he said glumly. "The more data we can send to headquarters, the better."

Portia nodded. "I've more samples to run." Her gaze settled on the table in front of the armchair. She'd rested her cuppa there last night without noticing it, while reading those boring articles of local news….

She stood motionless, lips parted.

"You got something?" McAdams asked. "Tell me."

Her head snapped up. "Does the sequencing lab stock ferret primers?"

"Ferrets?"

"There are enough pet ferrets around the town for someone to make their quid selling bespoke ferret accessories."

"What? Like little footy jerseys?" McAdams combed his fingers through his graying hair. His bulging eyes turned thoughtful. "Ferrets are carnivores. The company hasn't coded an instinct to hunt them into the strallos and ozraptors." Behind him, the esky pinged. He took his cup and saucer, then aimed his head down the corridor to the sequencing lab. "Ready? You need your morning tea."

"I'll get my cuppa while we amplify ferret DNA." She led the way. The soles of her boots thumped vinyl tile. Though her fingers trembled, she powered up the sequencer and extracted a DNA solution from the next swab without spilling.

[I need ferret primers,] she asked the sequencer.

A *bong* sounded in a minor key. Red words floated in the air above the machine. *Species not found.*

Portia wrinkled her nose. A quick lookup through her neury of the scientific name. [Primers for *Mustela putorius*.]

*Species not found. Did you mean **Mus musculus**?*

She mashed her lips together, then spat words at the sequencer. "If I wanted the common mouse I would have asked for it."

McAdams cleared his throat. "The sequencer doesn't have ferret primers?"

Warmth flushed her cheeks. "No, sadly. Can we order it from the local shire's molecular fabrication utility?"

"From my experience," McAdams said, "We have the needed scientific or medical clearances. If the local fab has DNA synthesis capability."

"How could it not?"

McAdams lowered his tea cup from his lips. "It's a small town. Try, of course, but temper your expectations."

She passed between lab benches to the windows. Low in the northeastern sky, Stella Australis A threw its red-orange light over tidy neighborhoods and the crowns of elms and oaks. The local fab lay about two klicks to the west. Not even its cooling towers and tank farms could be seen.

Portia accessed the local fab's order server through her neury. [A standard set of DNA amplification primers for ferret, please.]

Her neury showed her the fab's reply in a word balloon projected into her vision over the fab's site. *I'm sorry, I don't have a DNA synthesizer. The nearest facility that can process your request is in Centennial City.*

[That's three hundred klicks away!]

They can deliver it for free by ground in two days or by air tomorrow before fourteen o'clock, if you'll pay the rush delivery fee.

Fiddlesticks. Portia took a calming breath. [We'll pay the rush fee.] With a thought, she sent a funds request to the company's accounting systems.

Five seconds later, motion made her turn her head. Black letters on the off-white wall. —Request denied.—

"Can you talk to acco?" Portia asked McAdams. "I'm trying to order rush delivery from Centennial City and accounting shut me down."

"They'll cut my grass too," McAdams said. "Standard delivery?"

"Day after tomorrow."

He rolled his shoulders. "She'll be apples," he said, a touch of dejection in his mild voice. "Till then, we'll at least be able to rule out other animals." He raised an eyebrow. A smirk tightened his cheeks. "After you run more samples."

With a scowl, she pulled the next swab from the coldbox. Yes, she had to run the next sample, but it would come up as empty as the others. She rolled her lips together as she injected the DNA solution into the sequencer. Amplification started. At least an hour to wait....

A thought perked her up. She would put the time to use.

Five minutes later, she stood on the sidewalk outside the lab building with a lidded paper cup of tea. A warm breeze came from the north. Almost mild enough weather to shuck her jacket, and a harbinger of the summer to come. Her rideshare sedan pulled up and she climbed in.

"Where to?" said the self-driving car's bland voice.

She double-checked the news article from her neury, then gave the address of the custom pet accessories shop.

The rideshare delivered her to a block of single-story buildings fronted with brick and glass. Tucked between an acupuncturist and a sports pub showing cricket highlights, the pet shop's front window showed mannequin dogs and cats wearing Halloween costumes and eating or drinking from fine porcelain bowls engraved with *Rover* and *Fluffy*.

Two steps on the sidewalk. A bell rattled as Portia went in. The interior smelled of household pets, dogs and cats and ones more exotic. Display tables showed dog collars. Along one side wall, hamsters squeaked in a habitat of wooden platforms and exercise wheels.

A proprietress came from around a counter. At first glance, not much older than Portia, the proprietress wore her red hair in a ponytail bobbing behind her round face. With a breathy voice, she said, "I'm afraid we aren't equipped for dinos. Yet."

Portia squinted, then her eyes relaxed. The proprietress saw the company's logo on her shirt. "I'm actually here about a ferret."

The proprietress's turn to look puzzled. "I'd always heard you lot couldn't keep pets, spending summers here and winters up the big smoke."

"We can't." Part of Portia wanted to keep her voice nonchalant, but the rest of her saw the minnie dying of thirst over her broken eggs. "It's very important. I'm here to find out if anyone released a ferret into the preserve. It's an invasive species and—"

The proprietress backed off a step. Her face turned wary.

Portia slowed her voice. "I'm not looking to get anyone in trouble. All I want is info to help us keep the preserve a safe place for the dinosaurs."

"What harm could a ferret cause to some bonzer dino?"

"Attacking its eggs."

A gasp. The proprietress's round face paled. "Holy dooley. I'll help. What do you need to know?"

"Do you sell ferrets?"

The proprietress shook her head. "We don't sell any animals."

"Where would someone from here buy a ferret?"

"The nearest registered breeder is up near Centennial City. People can also buy them from other owners."

Portia rubbed the side of her nose. No way to track private sales. But on the other hand... "Can you share the breeder's name and number?"

"I'll send it now."

The contact information seemed to hover near Portia's ear. After it passed a virus scan, her neury stored it in her silicon subconscious.

"I'd also like info on your customers who've bought ferret accessories."

"Coming up."

Seconds later, that data joined the ferret breeder's contact in the back of her mind. "Thank you for your time. If I have more questions, would you mind if I come back?"

"Mind? Holy dooley, of course not. I want what's best for all animals."

Portia thanked her and left. On the ride back to the field office, she fed the customer list to a mapping program. Blue dots littered the countryside across parts of three shires.

When she ranked them by proximity to the minnie's smashed nest, one stood out. Bruce Fowler, on a farm about two klicks north of the preserve boundary. A malicious foe of the preserve? Or an unlucky victim of his pet's escape from its cage?

In the lab building, at the top of the stairs, McAdams waited with folded arms. "I thought you were working." His booming voice echoed down the hall.

Portia smiled through his interrogation. "While the sequencer's amplifying the next sample, I got a lead." She told him about her trip to the pet accessories shop.

"Not bad work. Though the real culprit might never have overpaid for that sheila's custom pet piffle."

"I'll call up the breeder next." Through her neury, she checked the sequencer's status report. Two minutes to go. "After I get the next sample into the sequencer."

After the morning's first sequencing run ended, she swept the negative results out of the air with a wave of her hand, then called. The breeder looked a decade older than McAdams, but handsome enough for his age, with a trimmed black beard and clear skin. Thin lips made him look wary to begin with, even before she mentioned the possible release of ferrets on the preserve.

He leaned away from the camera. His hand covered his mouth and nose. Through his fingers, he said, "I take customer privacy seriously... required all legal like... my solicitor will contact you, Miss, Doctor... G'day." His image broke into fragments that vanished.

Portia mashed her lips together. He'd lied, hadn't he? His solicitor would never call. Through her neury, she dictated a note for McAdams to append to the report. For the company to get a list of the ferret breeder's customers might require *its* solicitor.

She calmed herself with a breath. Enough of video calls. She had enough time before the second run finished to take action in real life.

Portia rapped on the open door of McAdams' office. "The ferret breeder pulled an american on me."

"Don't call him, his lawyer will call you? I'll put that in the report. Headquarters can investigate further."

Portia raised her chin. "So can we. The second sequence is running. Bruce Fowler, the farmer with the ferret, lives only forty klicks south of here. Fifteen minutes in the quaddy."

McAdams' eyes bulged even more than usual. "You've got a lot of zeal, Doctor, but accounting will be on you like flies on—manure."

"It's company business."

"It's not urgent enough."

"Don't you want to get to the bottom of this?"

"D'you hear what I'm saying? Of course I do. We'll talk to Fowler. By driving down after quitting time."

Portia's long fingers jittered, as if pent-up energy sought ground by playing an invisible piano. Another calming breath. "That will do."

"And who knows? Maybe a sequence will hit before then."

None did. Five minutes after twenty-four o'clock, she and McAdams joined the tail of the queue of field office employees waiting for rideshares. A small sport ute with knobby tires and a kangaroo bar jutting out between the headlights rolled up for them. They drove into downtown Tallis, then south on an asphalted shire road that turned to gravel five klicks out of town. The sun threw the sport ute's long, dust-blurred shadow ahead and to the left. Gravel rattled under the wheels. The sport ute's stiff suspension carried each bump to her in high fidelity.

Finally, after an hour and a turn onto an even bumpier side road, they came to Fowler's farm. A grid of small paddocks held herds of riddlepigs, each one hosting cloned organs for transplant into a human. A thousand meters off the side road, a long, low house sprawled across a swell in the terrain. An asphalt driveway led from the side road to the house. The tires whispered and Portia eased into her seat.

"He can afford custom pet kit, can't he?" McAdams said.

"How do you mean?"

"Have you seen any other paved lanes out this way?"

They pulled up at the house. Subtle signs of prosperity everywhere, now that she knew to look for them. A children's jungle gym and fort big enough for a school playground in one side yard. Under a gazebo seeming to float on slender nanotube alloy poles, an L-shaped outdoor kitchen could service a restaurant. When Portia and McAdams climbed out, the stink of hundreds of wallowing riddlepigs made her nose wrinkle.

"Smell of cryptoquid," McAdams said. He gestured with his chin and they walked up a flagstone path to the front door. Under a slanted awning, next to a narrow sand garden unraked for days, he aimed his hand at the doorbell button, but Portia beat him to it.

Chimes bonged behind frosted glass windows. Moments later, the door swung open. Out came the smells of stir-frying onions, soap, and eucalyptus vapor. The latter came from the vape pen held by the man waiting inside. Tall but slouched, with narrow ears, a thin mustache, and chewed fingernails, he wore clean clothes and hair still damp from a shower.

"We're with the dinosaur company," Portia said, "and we'd like to speak with Bruce Fowler."

The man blinked heavily, then puffed on his vape pen. His voice sounded squeaky. "That's my son. What's this about?"

"We'd like to ask him about his ferret."

Fowler exhaled a stream of vapor at her, then looked up at McAdams. "Why does the dino preserve need to know about my son's pet?"

Portia mashed her lips together. McAdams spoke. "We're looking at leasing a dozen hectares from a farmer hereabouts for a staging area. Mostly for storing equipment, but we would build a dino enclosure for animals coming on or going off the preserve. Part of our due diligence is to enquire about pets. We want minimum risk of a dino harming them."

A nibble on a fingernail, then a nod from Fowler. Calculation showed in his eyes. "The loss of a dozen hectares would hit me in the pocketbook, but I'm sure the company would make me whole. And we won't let my son's pet stop us from striking a deal. Come in. Have a seat. I'll get my son."

Fowler stepped out of the doorway and gestured at the room beyond. A sprawling room under a slanted ceiling, lit by red-orange sunlight through quadrilateral windows, floored in clacking wood the color of honey. Low furniture, straight lines, black leather and chrome, like museum pieces taken from the original Sydney Opera House... littered with bright plastic toys, a half-complete jigsaw puzzle, and empty beer cans. McAdams plopped down on a sofa. Careful of needles, Portia moved a cross-stitch project of cartoon children praying *Bless this Mess* off the cushion to a coffee table, then sat herself.

The farmer went off, toward the smell of onions and the sizzle of stir-fry. Young children shrieked and a woman's muffled voice carried from the kitchen.

Portia's stomach rumbled. She inhaled, then said by neury, [A good thought to lie to him.]

[You catch more flies with an open mouth,] McAdams said, then looked up.

Fowler entered with a teenaged boy. The family resemblance was plain in height and shape of head. The boy had smooth skin and a matching confidence in his eyes. The kind of boy who'd run his hands up a girl's skirt. Who'd make girls want him to. He shook an antique wristwatch, stainless steel and glass, past the cuff of his sleeve, then extended his other hand to McAdams. "Bruce Fowler." He turned to shake Portia's. While smiling breezily, he said, "How'd you do, Miss?"

Portia cooled her voice. "Dr. Oakeshott."

"These folks are with the dino company," Mr. Fowler said. "They're asking about your ferret."

A frown creased Bruce Fowler's smooth face. "My ferret?" A moment later, he chuckled. "Oh, Doctor, Mr. McAdams, you drove all the way from town for nothing."

"You don't have a ferret?" Portia asked.

"Not anymore. Turned out he was a right nippy bastard. Maybe he would've been milder if I'd had him gelded? No matter."

A dark sensation gnawed at Portia's stomach. "You sold him?" she asked, praying the answer was *yes*.

"Couldn't. No one was interested."

Mr. Fowler's squeaky voice broke in. "Not even that sheila down the road?"

Portia turned to the older man with dread chilling her face. *How could a father not know that his own son had got rid of a pet?*

"Which one?" Bruce Fowler asked. "Oh, Callie. Nah, she got sick of hers same time I did of mine."

In her own ears, Portia's voice seemed to come from far off. "What did you and Callie do with your ferrets?"

"One night, oh, two weeks it's been, dead of winter. Her parents had gone up to Centennial for a night away and she got her younger sibs to bed. We took the ferrets out to her back paddock and shooed them away."

Portia's throat caught. McAdams spoke. "Her back paddock."

"Yeah. Butting up on the dino preserve. We figured a strallo or an ozraptor would munch them up." Bruce Fowler quirked his mouth from side to side. "Oh, bugger, did they make a dino sick?"

"No." Portia managed to say one more thing. "Was Callie's ferret a female? Unspayed?"

"Yeah, maybe." The teenager gave her a look of honest innocence. "What of it?"

Mr. Fowler took another puff of his vape pen. "Clearly, there's no ferret issue to keep us from coming to the deal we talked about."

Portia's stomach knotted. She turned away and breathed deeply. God willing her bile would stay down.

"That does move you up the list," McAdams said. "Sounds like dinner's nearly ready. Thanks for your time. We'll see ourselves out." He tapped Portia's shoulder blade. She trudged with him to the door.

Outside, the sport ute squatted, backdropped by the fields of Fowler and his neighbor, and the deep green Cretaceous forest at the preserve's outer perimeter three thousand meters away.

"At least we know the problem," McAdams said. "Headquarters will come up with a solution. Engineer tougher minnie eggs, add an instinct to hunt ferrets to the predators, something."

Portia couldn't speak. Her gaze roved the deep green forest, looking for the minnie who'd lost her clutch, and all the others.

KUNBARRA AND THE WHITEANTS

KUNBARRA AND THE WHITEANTS

The motorcoach rolled through the shadowed streets of the town at the bottom of the world.

That's what the advertising transponders called it, in between the times they hawked hotels, restaurants, and tourist attractions by pinging Portia Oakeshott's neuronal interface. Overlaid on her vision of one-story brick-fronted shops and smooth concrete sidewalks played videos of hot air balloon rides, a waterpark, the British history museum—all the sights in and around Blenheim. Except for the dinosaur preserve about thirty kilometers south of town.

At least the transponders knew she and everyone on the bus were dinosaur workers, not tourists.

Portia nestled deeper against the padded backrest. The seat's servos murmured to conform the padding to her body while a pop singer crooned in her mind's ear. Almost a full workday, ten hours on the bus to cross the thousand klicks from Port Bounty on the continent's north coast. The firewagon, some wit had called it when they'd boarded that morning. All hands on deck. The company's biggest rollout of dinosaur eggs in a decade.

Over a thousand, mostly mickeys and kunbarras, two similar herbivorous species covered with bony plates. The latest versions from the gene jocks had thicker egg casings and an instinct to bury them deeper into the preserve's rich soil, farther from the reach of small predators. Incubated to within a week of hatching at the company's Port Bounty headquarters, the eggs flew down earlier that day in the cargo holds of the company's biggest quadrotor aircraft, while the crews that would place the eggs in the field rode down. In comfort, yes, with snacks, tea, and coffee on demand from the esky and a well-ventilated loo for after the free drinks ran their course.

Still, a long day. Knowing only a couple of klicks remained in their journey made her impatient to get to the hotel. What took so long? Blenheim had an afternoon rush hour, believe it or not, but she'd driven through it before. Traffic shouldn't be as heavy as this.

The motorcoach turned. The brakes gave a pneumatic hiss. Her upper body swung a few centimeters off the backrest.

The bus came to a halt.

From the row in front of her, a field ecologist muttered, "What the bloody hell?"

She rolled her lips together at the indelicate language. Then something made her pause her music. A crowd's voices, words indistinct from distance and the motorcoach's insulated windows. A chant in a millennium-old rhythm of petulant protest.

Portia leaned forward and rested her hand on seat back in front. "Can you make out what they're saying?"

The field ecologist turned to her a face dominated by a high forehead and a pair of sunglasses. "Nah, Doctor."

She sat back and used her neury to pipe sound from the bus' external microphone to her auditory nerves.

The crowd's chant became clear. "Hey hey ho ho, dinos are abomino!"

She rubbed the side of her nose and darted glances around. Her coworkers in surrounding rows all had the look of listening in. All looked nervously to one another.

"Hey hey ho ho, dinos are abomino!"

The bus rolled a car-length forward, then stopped.

"Who the hell are they?" asked the field ecologist.

"Sounds like religious nutters, mate," said another male voice.

"Twenty-four-sevens?" the field ecologist said.

Portia spoke up. "No. To them, we're sinners because we don't keep Sunday of Earth's week as the sabbath. What we do with fossil evidence, bird and reptile DNA, simulations, and guesswork doesn't mean a whit to them."

The field ecologist looked over the back of his seat. Reflected in his sunnies were a hurricane fence and a nanotube alloy building frame. "Which religious nutters, then?"

Portia shrugged. "There's enough empty around here for a hundred cults to settle." Another thought came to mind. "Or maybe they came down from Port Bounty, or one of the big cities on Cookland."

"Hey hey ho ho, dinos are abomino!"

A third thought came. She shivered and pulled her arms together.

A dozen motorcoaches a day came into Blenheim during New New South Wales' weeks of summer. How did the protestors know this bus carried company employees? And to which hotel it traveled?

The motorcoach lurched forward, one car length at a time. The chant grew louder. She could make out the words through her own ears. Around her, her coworkers craned their necks to look for the protestors.

Another five meters forward. The chant broke up into ragged roar. A crowd fanned out along both sides of the bus. All wore plain clothes in shades of gray and black, sleeves to wrists, pants cuffs and skirt hems to ankles. Trimmed beards on the men. The women wore scarves knotted at the neck, covering their ears and most of their hair. Righteous anger distorted the faces of either sex. Men and women alike shook raised fists.

Louder than ever. "Hey hey ho ho, dinos are abomino!"

Portia pulled her arms tighter. Could they rock the bus over?

Blue and red lights flickered on the ceiling and the edges of headrests near the windows. The lights grew more intense, dancing on the sides of the protestor's faces. From somewhere behind the bus, a siren gave an abbreviated bark.

Protestors turned to look. The chant wavered.

Portia leaned toward the window and peered in the right direction, but couldn't see the source of the siren.

A deep voice boomed from a megaphone. "This is the City of Blenheim Police Department. Interfering with traffic on a public street is a violation of city ordinance. Remove yourselves to the sidewalk or you'll be arrested."

The chant stopped. Protestors looked to one another, to the police, and to one of their own. A man, he looked not much older than Portia, thirty standard at the most, and clad all in black. Dirty blond hair parted on the left, and hazel eyes holding a mix of fanaticism and shrewdness.

The man raised his hand and beckoned the protestors toward him. He opened his mouth. His voice, surprisingly gravelly coming from his smooth face, carried through the bus' insulated windows. "Brothers, sisters, we render unto Caesar. The Lord shall see us to triumph at the time of His choosing."

With measured steps, the protestors stepped back to the curb. Portia let out a long breath, though she still warily watched the crowd. The anger recently on their faces had turned, but how quickly could it turn back?

Then she saw a woman with green eyes. Wisps of coal-black hair peeped under her scarf. The lines of her cheekbones, the upturned nose, she looked familiar. From uni? That girl who lived down the hall in Portia's final year. What was her name? Sally? Sandra.

Portia's nose wrinkled. Sandra had been a girl of colorful, skimpy attire and questionable virtue. Rumor had it she'd sneaked a boy into her room one night when her roommate was away. That couldn't be her, in a dour dress, four thousand klicks and three standard years from campus.

Could it?

The bus rolled forward. The chant resumed, louder than before. Sandra stood next to the man in black. They and the others watched the bus go with unreadable eyes.

. . .

The next morning, protestors lined the street as the motorcoach left the hotel, bound for the field office amid farmland two klicks south of Blenheim. Portia studied the crowd but Sandra eluded her eye.

That she'd seen her classmate she lacked all doubt. The night before, keyed up and unable to fall asleep, she searched the alumni forum. A year prior, Sandra Nithercott had changed her profile picture. No makeup, gray dress and scarf. *I've set aside my sins and found peace and joy with the Siblinghood.* The profile stated she lived in a small town in the Bagehot Hills of northern Blighland, eight hundred klicks from here.

More searching found a page about the Siblinghood. The commune eked out its quid by handcrafting pottery and wooden furniture, under the spiritual leadership of Brother Lucas Ruthven. A photo showed Ruthven in black and with dirty blond hair parted on the left.

One mystery solved, but another came to mind.

Why did the Siblinghood protest the company?

The bus pulled in at the field office, and a third mystery pressed out her other concerns. A sport ute in Blenheim PD colors parked with blinking lights near a windowless, two-story building of corrugated metal near the back of the grounds. The hangar. Yellow crime scene tape wrapped the building, with an extra strip of tape across the rolling doors.

"What did those mangy bastards do now?" muttered the field ecologist with the sunnies.

After debarking, they soon found out from the field office's operations manager. During the night, someone had stolen the rotors of every quaddy in the hangar. Neatly dismantled and removed, not just from the hangar, but from the entire grounds. The quaddies wouldn't fly until replacements were fabbed and remounted. The latter had to wait for the police forensics team to hoover up every scrap of evidence.

From the back of the crowd, Portia squinted across the grounds. Black half-domes of cameras dotted the hangar. "Surely we have video of the perpetrators," she called out.

The operations manager shook his jowly head. "The grounds lost main power last night. The backup generator failed to kick in. We found all the lines severed this morning. The police think the hoodlums used drones to knock out power, then did their work."

Power knocked out for hours. Portia gasped. "The kunbarra eggs!"

"Were covered in self-adjusting insulation. They stayed within temperature tolerances even with the loss of controlled ambient. We're a little cross at the overnight vet in the incubator for sleeping through everything." A wry smile softened the words. "Luckily, no one and no eggs were hurt."

A man's nasal voice barely carried from the front of the crowd. "It's obviously the religious fanatics what did this."

The ops manager rubbed the bags under his eyes. "Obviously, but the police still have to gather proof."

"When can we deploy the eggs?" asked the field ecologist with the sunnies and high forehead.

"We'll push for today, but if I were a punter, I'd bet against it. We ordered rotors from the municipal fab, right. But we have to wait for the police to finish before the mechanics can get started. Then the quaddies need test flights before the mechanics will cert them for use." He gave a grin. "But I reckon we can find a task around here for every jack and jill of you."

He was right. For a few hours. But by seventeen o'clock, local noon, Portia had finished checking the dispensary for expired medication. She joined the rest of the crew milling about on the parking lot and adjoining lawn. Some of the men played cricket with a broom and a ball made from duct tape. A glance past them, into the hangar, showed mechanics climbing up ladders and disassembling rotor housings. Strangers, bulky men wearing untucked shirts, swiveled their heads, ignoring the company employees, their gazes on the perimeter fence.

Between bowled balls, an ecologist playing deep midwicket told her in a scratchy voice, "Hired security. Company flew them in from Centennial City an hour back. They'll be on-site round the clock."

The ops manager's voice called across the parking lot from the front steps of the main building. "Hullo, what's this?"

The batsman shrugged with the broom in his hands. "We're all done with our tasks."

"You're all—" Even from a distance, the ops manager's jowly face showed surprise. "Crikey. Right, here's an update. The mechanics just informed me they need two flights eighteen hours apart to cert each quaddy. They cannot get that done today. So we're sending you back to the hotel."

Cheers sounded from the cricket players. Two blocks away, the motorcoach turned the corner for the field office.

"Don't get too much a gutful tonight. The motorcoach will pick you up tomorrow at twelve-thirty, and God help you if you're late."

Everyone filed aboard in good spirits. Who didn't want a paid day off? The kunbarra eggs wouldn't hatch for a few days yet. Fly them out tomorrow. No chant could stop a quaddy.

A chill ran down Portia's throat.

Would the Siblinghood escalate from chants to homemade missiles?

The bus rolled out the gate. On the far side of the road, against a backdrop of a hops field, eight Siblinghood members stood like ghosts in black and gray. Silent till now, they chanted in unison. Their voices lingered in Portia's mind long after the bus moved out of earshot.

More protestors waited for them at the hotel. They formed two lines flanking the entryway, barely farther apart than the bus was wide. The bus crept past contorted faces less than half a meter from Portia's window. The chant sounded louder than ever. "Hey hey ho ho, dinos are abomino!"

Heart racing, she scanned the faces for Sandra Nithercott, but didn't find her.

Finally, the motorcoach squeezed through the protestor gauntlet. Blenheim PD and more private security, hired by the company or the hotel, stood in clusters of two or three on the parking lot. They all looked to be suffering heartburn as their gazes roved the protestors.

The bus pulled up under the front awning. A company employee, a mousy woman with plump cheeks, waited for them. Her voice carried surprisingly well. "I'm beaming each of you a twenty cryptoquid voucher good for the hotel's restaurant and lounge."

The man with the nasal voice spoke. "You're telling us we have to stay on site?"

"You're grownups. We can't make you stay here. But with twenty quid in your pocket, why go anywhere else?"

The employees strode in. A typical lobby of a small town hotel, plastic plants, a bored young woman looking up in surprise from the front desk, a freshwater aquarium instead of a fountain. Most of the crowd headed left, toward the bar. Portia veered to the right.

"Doctor." The field ecologist had pushed his sunnies up his high forehead. He waggled his wrist as if it held a glass. "Having a pint?"

She smiled politely. "Not just yet. I need to look something up."

In her room, she sprawled on the bedspread and gazed idly at an impressionist print of kangaroos on the wall above the headboard. She rolled her lips together once. A good idea?

What harm could come of it?

Portia nodded to herself, then dictated a message through her neury.

To: sandra.nithercott@alumni.ueb.edu.nnsw

I got quite the surprise, looking out the bus window yesterday and seeing you here in Blenheim. Would like to know more about your position and tell you more about mine. Free today?

[Send,] she told her neury through nerve impulses rerouted away from her voicebox.

She waited for ten minutes, until a rumble in her stomach reminded her to eat lunch. In the hotel restaurant, she sat with a caprese salad. The balsamic vinegar lacked punch but the basil leaves surprised her with freshness. She washed down a bite with a sip of hot tea when an alert popped up in the lower right corner of her vision. *New message from sandra.nithercott@alumni.ueb.edu.nnsw.*

Portia opened it and read.

I thank the Lord our paths have crossed. Brother Lucas and I would love to meet you. We've camped at a ground east of town. A virtual card gave the full address, down to the site number. *Can you come to us this evening, twenty-six o'clock?*

She sipped her cuppa, composed her reply.

Till then.

. . .

At half past twenty-five, after changing out of her company uniform, she stopped in the hotel lounge and told people she was heading off site for a couple of hours. She gave the campground address.

"What's there?" asked a woman with the precise enunciation of the mostly drunk.

"The Siblinghood. The protestor cult."

The man with the nasal voice cut in. "Why'n the bloody hell are you visiting the enemy?"

"Don't I destroy my enemies when I make them my friends?"

Portia went to the back of the hotel. The door recognized her as a hotel guest and unlocked itself. Her rideshare waited on a strip of living asphalt facing the tall wooden privacy fences backing a residential neighborhood. She walked around the entire car. A nondescript sedan with the side and rear windows tinted dark.

She tossed a clutch purse onto the front seat, then climbed in and curled up next to it. Below line of sight of any casual glance through the windshield. The scents of new car and vat-grown leather comforted her.

The sedan rolled around the hotel. Seen through the tinted windows, the private security men watched the parking lot entrance and didn't give her a second glance.

A block away, Portia moved to the rear seats and sat up for the rest of the ride to the campground. The evening sun sent the car's shadow ahead of her. The sedan slowed, making her frown in puzzlement. A line of sweetgum trees screened the facility's entrance from the road.

A paved lane led past a concrete block building housing the front desk and gift shop. A teenaged boy wearing a polo shirt with the campground logo stood on the pavement and raised his hand. He leaned down and from under a sheaf of disheveled brown hair peered at her. Neury to neury, he said, [Checking in or visiting?]

[Visiting.]

The boy grimaced. [We won't stop you, but mind, we don't want trouble coming in or going out.]

[I'll give you none. Which way to site 14?]

His grimace remained as he gave directions and pointed. He stepped aside and the sedan rolled on. A left turn, then past RVs parked on gravel and down a hill toward a gully. Along the bank, branches of oaks and maples rustled over rows of tents.

She studied everything. No telling what detail might be important to help the company overcome the Siblinghood. *And bloody hell, record what you see and hear to your neury.* She gave the commands and heat drained from her cheeks.

Just past a concrete block building with signs for mens' and womens' and the guest laundry, two men in gray and black stopped her car. The one with the slender build and crewcut spoke. [Your name and your purpose?]

[Portia Oakeshott. I'm here to visit—there she is.]

Sandra glided toward them, her skirts rustling the pavement. "I've invited her to meet Brother Lucas," she said, voice warm. Her green eyes met the gaze of the crewcut guard. A private conversation over their neuries, obviously.

Sandra turned to Portia. "Park here, then come with me."

Portia did as bade, then climbed out, clutch purse in hand. The summer air felt warm on her bare elbows and her ankles exposed by her crop pants. How could Sandra stand being smothered in her thick, dark skirts?

"You look good," she said, to say something. A closer look and then she noticed a glow in Sandra's full cheeks.

Sandra beamed. "You see it. The Lord has blessed me with a healthy pregnancy, so far."

A glance down, no baby bump. "How far along?"

"Three standard months." Sandra's green eyes crinkled. Her gaze darted to Portia's bare ring finger. "No children for you yet?"

"We have hundreds of kunbarra eggs to lay out on the preserve."

Sandra's smile dripped sweet condescension. "In time you'll find that isn't remotely the same." She scratched under her head scarf, just above her ear, and Portia recalled she'd often worn jangling hoop earrings. "I remember you were a veterinary major, but what led you to work on dinosaurs?"

Her tone gave Portia pause. She hadn't thought about Sandra's agenda, but now it seemed obvious. Gather intel from Portia, if not convert her outright. So Portia set aside the true answer—a childhood playing with plastic dinos in her suburban bedroom had planted the seed of a passion—and said with a rueful tone, "The pay is good."

"And?"

"My then-boyfriend took a job with the company. I followed because I thought we loved each other."

Sandra's mouth opened as if to ask further. Sweat trickled in Portia's underarms and she wished she'd applied more anti-perspirant from the tiny stick in her clutch purse. God willing Sandra wouldn't pry for more details on which young man at uni had been her non-existent boyfriend.

"The only love which never wavers is the Lord's. Here we are."

The tent looked like a small house with guy lines. Angled sunlight through the trees gave a glow to panels of yellow and orange. From the panels, Portia judged the tent had two side rooms off the main. An LED lantern hung unused over the door, which dangled loosely in the breeze. Coiled flaps let air into screened windows.

Another guard stood midway between a cold firepit and a canopy over a picnic table. His pendulous ears wobbled as he turned his head to Sandra. "This is her?"

"Yes, brother."

He set his hands on his hips and jutted out his elbows. He narrowed his eyes at Portia, but after a moment his expression softened. "The Lord faults no one for ignorance. Brother Lucas will speak to you of truth." He stepped aside and turned. With one hand he gestured toward the tent.

Portia walked that way over dirt and patchy grass. The guard's gaze never left her face. Her fingers tightened on her clutch purse. She would almost prefer the guard's eyes dart to her figure, as every man, no matter how pious, was wont to do from time to time.

She kept her thoughts off her face and went by the guard with a single nod of her head.

Sandra stepped around Portia and pulled the door flap back about five centimeters. "Brother Lucas?" she said through the gap, voice soft and warm.

Lucas Ruthven cleared a little gravel from his throat, but not much. "Enter, little sister, and Dr. Oakeshott."

Sandra held the flap fully open. Portia entered without needing to stoop. Her grip tightened on the clutch purse. Her coworkers knew her location and police forensics caught every criminal. Still, she entered a lion's den.

Ruthven stood near the back of the tent with his hands behind his back. His hazel eyes regarded her and how much gel did he put in his dirty blond hair to keep his part so sharp all day?

Set aside your nerves and focus on what's important.

"G'day, Doctor."

Portia extended her hand. "G'day, Mister—Reverend—Brother—?"

"Brother Lucas, if you please." Ruthven gave her hand a cool look. "No offense, but other than in service to the Lord, I touch no woman but my wife."

Portia dropped her hand and gave a gracious smile. "I respect your ways, Brother Lucas." Inwardly, she seethed. As if *she* were a harlot lusting after *him*.

To cover her thoughts, she glanced toward a sound from the side room to her left. Someone shifting his or her body. For a moment, a bright shaft of sunlight threw a silhouette onto the orange plastic wall. Mannish shoulders, close-cropped hair, upturned nose and bearded jaw. Obviously not Ruthven's wife.

Then who?

Ruthven cleared his throat. He extended his hand toward a stool near the door and two steps to Portia's left. "Doctor, have a sit, if you please."

Portia took a seat on a thin cushion. Though slender as styluses, the stool's nanotube alloy legs held her weight. Sandra sat on a stool to the right of the door. Ruthven lowered himself to one near the back wall. The three of them formed a triangle facing one another. Portia's nape crawled with the realization that someone lurked no more than two meters behind her.

"What brought you to visit us, Doctor?"

Portia gestured at Sandra. "I looked out the window yesterday and saw a familiar face." She turned to Ruthven's hazel eyes. "It made me want for us to get to know each other better. Perhaps we can find some common ground—"

"We cannot compromise with sin, Doctor."

She blinked. "I, your words, what exactly do you mean that 'dinosaurs are abominations'?"

"The meaning should be plain to one of my little sister's uni classmates."

"Yes, I suppose, what I mean, what makes them abominations or sins?"

"They are abominations because they are the fruits of your sins. You play god and the Lord will pass judgment. I pray that you repent before His judgment falls on you."

Portia rubbed the side of her nose. "I understand our techniques might be unfamiliar to the general public, but perhaps if I explain—"

"No explanation is needed," Ruthven said. "I majored in livestock science at North Blighland A & M. I well know all the techniques used in genetic engineering and ecoseeding."

"I don't understand."

"The Lord ordained that dinosaurs should pass from the universe sixty-five million years ago. Your company usurp the Lord's prerogative to decide which species live and which pass away. Do you understand now?"

Portia drew in a deep breath. Despite the smells of tent plastic and castile soap, her heart slowed and slid down from her throat. "I do."

Ruthven's hazel eyes softened. "Are you happy, Doctor?"

"Frankly, no. Come visit the preserve. I'll contact my superiors, perhaps a private guided tour. If you see them up close—"

"Not that," he said with a wave of his fingers. "Are you pleased living the life the king of the world tells you to live?"

She frowned. "What's Arthur II to do with anything?"

"The king of the material world, who took the Whore of Babylon as his consort." With a touch of exasperation, he said, "Satan."

Portia shuddered. "I live a Christian life."

Ruthven scowled. He opened his mouth to speak when Sandra leaned forward. "Brother Lucas, if I may?"

"Yes, little sister."

Sandra turned to Portia. Her head scarf framed her green eyes and her face lacking guilt and shame. "I know you didn't commit sins of the flesh in our uni days, and you look too much a lady for me to imagine you commit them now. Brother Lucas is instead talking about all the false things our society demands of you. You must get good grades. You must go to uni. You must find a good husband who has a good job. You must raise your children to repeat the cycle. And at the end, you wonder why your kitchen full of gadgets and your winter weeks at Capricorn Beach fail to make you happy."

She went on. "Strewth, they don't make anyone happy. Though the rich men who cannot pass through the eye of the needle fatten their cryptoquid accounts off you, they cannot fill the emptiness inside. And the men with reversed collars under vaulted ceilings and stained glass windows, who tell you the false things are God's will, feel their emptiness so much they secretly deny God exists. Why listen to them when you can listen to Brother Lucas?"

Portia's head swam in the stuffy air of the tent. Her head thrashed from Sandra to Ruthven and back. Sandra lied, of course. Ruthven was the man who demanded false things and claimed God wanted them. He had to be. Everything here had the sulfurous stink of a cult.

"You say so much," she said. "I really must go. Thank you for your hospitality but I really must go." On a hunch, she lowered her hand with the clutch purse below the seat of the stool and let go.

"Stay, sister. My words are a kookaburra's call compared to the truths Brother Lucas can tell you."

"No, I must, my coworkers, they know I'm here, I don't want them calling the police if I'm away too long—"

"You're free to go," said Ruthven in his gravelly voice. "And free to come back at the time of your choosing."

Sandra bowed her head to him. "You are indeed wise, Brother Lucas." She extended her arm and took Portia's hand. "Come, sister, I'll walk you to your car."

Portia followed Sandra out. Rows of tents stretched up the slope toward the restroom and laundry building. The guard with the pendulous ears gave Portia a wistful look. She gave him a smile to make her grandmother proud, then walked away.

How long should she wait?

Sandra helped her answer the question. Halfway to the waiting sedan, Sandra's mouth scrunched and a pained expression touched her green eyes. She rested her hand on her stomach. "I don't know why they call it morning sickness. It can strike anytime."

"That'd be right," Portia said. In a quiet voice, she added, "Oh dear."

"What's the matter?"

"You might suffer from some nausea, but at least you're free of the monthlies."

Sandra's eyes went wide with sympathetic understanding. "You don't take hormones to regulate or prevent it? That's pleasing to the Lord."

Portia looked down at her hands. "And I carried along—just in case —where did I leave my clutch?"

"You had it with you when we entered Brother Lucas' tent. Didn't you?"

"I did. I must have left it there." Her mouth turned down and she swung her head from Sandra to the tent down the slope.

"Go get it." Sandra winced and flattened her fingers on her mouth. "I can't go with you." She turned for the womens', her usual poise lost to shuffling feet and torso hunched over her stomach.

One of her handlers down. Portia went back downslope. A gaggle of low clouds masked the rays of Stella Australis A. In the slight gloom under the oaks' spread branches, the guard with the pendulous ears opened his mouth in a smile. "What brings you back, miss?"

"I was so engrossed by Brother Lucas' message that I forgot something. Mind if I go in and get it? Half a tick and I'll be out of his way."

"Of course. His messages engross us all."

Portia gave a half-smile over her shoulder. She approached the tent. The door flap was still unzipped. Soundlessly, she lifted it and stepped over the thin plastic threshold into the shaded interior, prepared to apologize to Ruthven for interrupting—

He wasn't in the main room.

She glanced around. Her clutch purse there, under her stool.

In which side room was Ruthven?

"She gives us an in to the company." His gravelly voice came from the left.

"Whatever." A harsh male voice with an odd, flat accent. Not from New New South Wales. Not even from any of the can-worlds and space stations in the Stella Australis system. "Tomorrow you start protesting the high-end hotels. Especially the Churchill, that's where most off-worlders stay. Make rich bitches clutch their pearls."

"If we work on the company's employees, we can further your objective and save their souls."

Portia picked up her purse and backed away.

The male voice grew harsher. "Who's paying your bills here—" He switched to an exaggerated strine accent. "—*mate*?"

With a faint rustle, her back and rump pushed aside the loose door flap. She held her breath until she lifted both her feet over the threshold and onto bare ground. She turned and strode quickly away.

"All's good?" the guard asked.

Portia waggled her purse, then touched a finger to her lips. "Brother Lucas is resting," she said softly.

The guard lowered his voice. "Right good of you to tell me."

"G'day," she said, and hurried up the slope. There, just past the restrooms and the two guards, her rideshare sedan. Get in, get out of here, before someone suspects.

A retching sound echoed off concrete block and out the doorway to the womens'. Sandra.

Portia's fingers stiffened around her clutch. What might Sandra tell Ruthven? *She said she had an urgent feminine issue. I'm surprised she rode back to her hotel to address it.*

Though part of her wanted to sprint to the rideshare, Portia overcame the urge. With quick steps, she entered the womens'. Beyond the mirror, sinks, and handsoap dispensers, Sandra's retching reverberated out of the first stall. Portia went to the last stall, giving a glance to the only window on the back wall, high, small, two panels of frosted glass of which one could be leaned out. Perhaps a gymnast or a lady spy could slip through, but she couldn't.

Portia closed the stall door behind her. Her nose wrinkled at the bite of bleach undercut by a mildewy odor from the showers. She crouched, not letting the seat of her pants touch the toilet. Her quads burned, but at least someone seeing her feet under the stall partition would assume she sat.

How long would it take to sell her story? She braced her hands, one on the concrete block wall and the other on the metal stall partition, until the burn in her quads forced her to stand.

With a tight feeling in her gut, she left the stall. None of Ruthven's guards blocked the entrance. Only Sandra, bent over a sink, shared the restroom with her.

Sandra straightened up. Water dripped down her pallid cheeks. She reached for a recyclable cloth handtowel that muffled her words as she blotted her face. "The Lord only made us bear these burdens to bring new life into the world because He knew we could manage them."

Portia smiled weakly. Quick bursts of water, soap, more water. She wrung a towel through her hands. If only she could ask Sandra about the man with the flat accent... but that would give the game away. "I wish you and your husband all the best with your baby."

"Please, sister, mind Brother Lucas' words. He speaks the truth, and happy are all those who hear."

"I will," Portia said. "G'day."

Two minutes later, the rideshare turned out of the campground's driveway and onto the main road back to Blenheim. A glance behind her showed no one followed. She gave a relieved sigh and pulled excerpts from her neury recording. As the sedan approached a half-completed development of new houses raised on stilts Queenslander style, she rang up John Pietrangelo, the company's chief operations officer.

Ten seconds for the call to bounce off a satellite and reach Port Bounty. A video window appeared between her and the sedan's windshield. Black hair low on his forehead, a lean and sharp face, wiry limbs. A tall boy on the schoolyard had probably mocked his short stature. Once.

A gray suit, a knotted yellow tie, and a bookcase behind him filled with golf memorabilia showed Pietrangelo was still in his office despite the late hour. "You aren't one to jump the chain of command willy-nilly, Dr. Oakeshott. What's come up?"

Her heard thumped. "I paid a visit to the Siblinghood's leaders."

"You did what?"

"I saw a familiar face among the protestors, an acquaintance from uni. I contacted her and she introduced me to the Siblinghood's leader."

He glanced to the side, checking data through his neury. "Lucas Ruthven?"

"Yes."

Black eyebrows knitted. "A moment ago you said 'leaders.'"

A smile pushed tight her cheeks. "I recorded some things you need to see. And hear."

"Send them."

She transferred the silhouette and the conversation between Ruthven and the man from outsystem. Pietrangelo sipped from a black mug of coffee and stared intently past her. "That's an American accent…. If it's from… I'll be stuffed."

Glinting dark eyes focused on Portia. "Good onya for finding this. I've got a hunch. I'll run this through an accent checker."

A moment later, Pietrangelo's eyes squeezed shut and he threw back his head. He guffawed from deep in his belly. "Mangy whiteant bastards!"

"Sir?"

His laughter died down enough to talk. "We called it 'whiteanting' where I grew up, around Anzac Cove. You don't know the word?"

"No."

"It's when someone plays unfair to bring down the competition. Hiring someone to post one-star reviews of your rival's products, things like that." Pietrangelo chuckled. "That bloke's wank-yank accent matches to New Minnesota."

"New Minnesota." Her eyebrows jumped. "Plastocine Park."

"Now, now, let's take the high road and call it by its proper name, 'Pleistocene Park.'"

She'd seen videos, of course. Sabertooth tigers prowling around herds of woolly mammoths. Hagerman horses galloping across a plain. Short faced bears, taller than a man, attacking giant tapirs. All running loose on a small continent, all reconstructed in part from preserved DNA. All extinct.

"They do the same thing the Siblinghood condemns us for." She didn't laugh but simply shook her head. "Mangy whiteant bastards, indeed."

"I'll forward this on to the Frontier Police. From the silhouette and the voice print, they can likely identify that bloke."

"And arrest him."

Pietrangelo grimaced. "Wager you five quid he's diplomatic personnel attached to the New Minn embassy. The frontos and I will have to lobby the Foreign Minister to have the bloke declared *non grata*. But that's not what's important."

"It isn't?" Portia asked.

"Not compared to knocking out Lucas Ruthven's cult."

"I see. He'd lose all credibility with his followers." Her voice sounded quiet in her ears. Cult or not, Sandra seemed happy enough with her new life.

"Who cares about them? Ruthven's credibility with tourists, especially off-worlders, will get smashed flat. That's all that matters."

"If I may, sir. No."

"No?"

She thought of newborn kunbarras, cracking their eggs open from the inside with pushes of their blocky heads. "What most matters is our dinos."

LOOVY AND THE LAVA

LOOVY AND THE LAVA

A gust of wind threw grit against the south-facing windows of the conference room. Portia Oakeshott rose from her seat at the long table and crossed to the nearest pane. She extended slender fingers toward grains skittering down the glass.

The lawn below the window, between the main building and the hangar, looked green. No accumulation. Yet? Beyond the hangar, the sky seemed overcast. A haze veiled barns and farmhouses normally visible along the ridgeline five klicks to the south.

"How are the particulates?" boomed the voice of Ridley McAdams, field ecologist. The others in the room, company personnel stationed here in Margarettown, echoed the question with crinkled eyebrows and nervous glances out the window.

"Barely a problem." Portia hugged her arms against her body. "Here." God knew what damage the eruption would inflict on the preserve. Giant ferns and palm-like cycad trees smothered in ash? Dinosaurs shrieking in pain, unable to escape flows of lava?

She turned away from the window. "Any news?"

McAdams snorted. "Twenty channels, and nineteen of them are journos earbashing without saying anything." His bulging eyes darted over the wall opposite the windows, where a four by five grid of video windows rose above the chair rail, projected onto their optic nerves by their neuronal interfaces, their neuries.

Portia sat. She rubbed the side of her nose and reached for her cuppa while her gaze roved the wall of video.

One channel cut to a journette in front of a satellite map. Her face had clear skin tighter than nature could manage. Behind her, a crinkly line of white and gray crossed the map horizontally. A call-out box of text identified one crinkle in the middle as Eighty-three. The journette said in a buttery voice, "So named for having an elevation bang-on 8300 meters and for straddling the 83° latitude line. The highest peak in the South Polar Range. A volcano long believed to be dormant, a belief proven utterly false...."

A dark green box covered most of the map from the mountain range to the top edge. The Blighland Dinosaur Preserve. Just below the top, a small circle around a gridded gray splotch labeled Margarettown.

Portia sipped and grimaced. Her tea had grown cold.

She regarded the map with another grimace. No scale. She knew the preserve's perimeter lay about four hundred kilometers north of Eighty-three, and Margarettown, about forty klicks north of the perimeter. But without a scale, someone who didn't know the region might think the volcano erupted right outside the town.

Someone? Mum. She'd call any minute now, wouldn't she? *It isn't safe out there. And if you transferred full-time to the company headquarters, perhaps you could find a good young man....*

"Where's a live feed?" muttered Ms. Southwark, the office manager, a woman comfortable with her lined face and wisping hair. She pulled the collar of her shirt away from her skin. She fanned her neck with one hand. Thin bracelets jangled while she squinted at the video wall. "There."

An aerial view from a quadrotor. The camera panned over the jumbled, dark green canopy of the preserve's Cretaceous forest. Here it covered lumpy foothills of the South Polar Range. The forest bathed in the rays of Stella Australis A, low in the northern sky. The cloud of ash and particulates had to be too high overhead to block the sun. The forest looked normal. Calming.

Until orange-red oozed into view like hot, congealing blood. A steaming, hissing lava flow scoured the hollows between foothills. It had come thousands of meters down Eighty-three's slopes. Though the lava had cooled since it gouted from the volcano, the flow might have thousands more to go. Heat shimmered the view. Over the buzz of the quaddy's four rotors, an exterior microphone picked up the groan and pop of trees caught in the flow, snapped off their roots, roaring into flame. The quaddy held station, taking in the hellish view.

The quaddy's pilot wasn't the only noteworthy member of the animal kingdom in the vicinity. From the forest below the quaddy sounded a high-pitched chitter, the frantic calls of a herd of loovies, individuals of the emu-sized, grazing *Diluvicursor*.

Portia rolled her lips together. Her gaze roved the scene. Where were the loovies? But all she saw were the crowns of cycads and ferns, writhing in the wind rushing toward the lava.

A clipped male voice. The quaddy pilot. "Descending for a better squizz."

The view grew larger. Portia could make out dark red spots riding the lava like trash on a river. Starting to cool. God willing it would solidify soon.

Motion away from the lava caught her eye. There, through the heat shimmer, a brown mass glimpsed between spasming fronds of a cycad. A loovy. It raised its head. Maybe she imagined its eyes wide in alarm and the ruff of stiff, feathery filaments standing up on its nape. It opened its mouth, but she couldn't hear if it called over the crackle of burning trees and the rush of wind.

The loovy whisked its long tail around and loped away on its two legs.

The view began to shake. The pilot's voice turned higher and less clipped. "Encountering turbulence above the lava flow." A breath of calm, then a shake morphed into wild swing. The normal unison whine of the rotors gave way to dissonant pulses as each one fought for the right amount of lift to keep the quaddy airborne.

"Damn, too much rough air." The rotors roared together. The lava flow shrank and slid from the center of the screen. "Autopilot wouldn't let me stay. Going up to a thousand meters and two-fifty away from the turbulence column."

The lava flow shrank further, turning into a trickle of malignance against the deep green of the Cretaceous forest.

"And this isn't the only lava flow." The camera panned up, tracking the forested foothills for a dozen klicks or more. Three reddish-orange fingers groped down the volcano's foothills, toppling trees and emitting clouds of foul vapor. "Huge eruption. Maybe the biggest since Man settled New New South Wales."

Southwark fanned herself more vigorously. "I hope everyone cleared the preserve on time."

Another video window showed a harried young man with the company's logo on the breast of his blue polo shirt. He stood in front of a building dignified by blocks of quarried stone. At the company's headquarters at Port Bounty, a thousand klicks to the north.

Portia switched her hearing to the young man as he spoke, presumably to an off-camera journo. "—gave an evacuation order as soon as we became aware of the eruption. In consultation with the best vulcanologists on the planet, we've expanded the evacuation zone as we've learned the eruption's full magnitude."

The journo was a journette with a voice smoothed down to Received Strine Pronunciation. "These summer weeks are your high season. How many tourists and employees were in the zone when the company gave the evacuation order?"

"We're still gathering that data."

The journette's voice smoothed further. Portia tensed her shoulders at a possible trap. "You don't know how many people were in the zone? How many might not have heeded the evacuation order?"

"It's my job to tell you what we know," said the spokesman. "Whatever you want to speculate is on you."

Employees around the table chuckled. A closed-mouth smile tightened Portia's face. *Good on you, telling off that muckraker.*

An alarm pinged in her mind's ear, and a notification popped into the lower left corner of her vision. *Incoming call from Pietrangelo, J.*

Pietrangelo? The company's chief operations officer? She'd spoken to him a few times during her three standard years with the company.

Why would he skip down the chain of command to talk to her? And on a day like this….

She straightened her back. [I'll take it,] she said to her neury.

Expecting a video window to overlay itself on her view of the room, her neury's reply surprised her. [Mr. Pietrangelo would like you to join a multi-person virtual environment.]

[He would?] But if anyone would have a good reason for such eccentricity, it would be the company's second in command. [Of course.]

A rush of sensation over her skin. She found herself sitting in one of the leather visitor chairs in Pietrangelo's corner office a thousand klicks to the north. A perfect simulation, down to the golfing knick-knacks on the shelves and the air conditioning raising gooseflesh on her forearms, while her body sat quietly in Margarettown and her neury completely swapped out the inputs from her senses.

On the other side of a wide desk of glossy brown wood sat John Pietrangelo. Black hair most of the way to his thick eyebrows. Suit a few shades of gray lighter than his hair and perfectly tailored to his short and athletic body, set off by a necktie striped in deep green and powder blue and a pocket square of the same striped silk. Portia often imagined that years prior, a playground bully called him a *wog prawn*. Once. Pietrangelo's wiry arms dished out black eyes and a fat lip for his trouble.

Pietrangelo's voice sounded as firm as his arms. "Southwark, McAdams, Dr. Oakeshott, good to see you. What I'm about to say stays between us."

The other two and Portia nodded or mumbled agreement. She sat between the other two, with Southwark on her right. Wait, Pietrangelo's office only had two visitor chairs, didn't it? But the proportions looked right. Some perspective trick induced by her neury in her optic nerve.

Southwark's bangled wrist dropped to her lap. "How can we help you, sir?"

"We've got a bugger of a mess and thank Christ the journos haven't gotten a hold of it. There's a small group, two tourists and a guide, who are within a thousand meters of a lava flow. They flew in by quaddy. The initial eruption sent rocks airborne and one of them, I reckon as wide as my desk—" He extended his arms and his fingertips couldn't reach the far sides. "—fell six thousand meters and smashed flat one of their quaddy's rotor arms."

Portia gasped. "That rock could've fallen on them."

"Good it didn't."

McAdams' voice boomed. "Where do we come in? You need us for a rescue?"

"That'd be right. Most of our emergency response assets are in Blenheim, with a few in Tallis." He named towns hundreds of klicks west and east, respectively, of Margarettown, and much farther from the flowing lava. "And those assets already deployed before we realized who those two tourists were out there, let alone who they were."

The gooseflesh on Portia's arms intensified. "Are they royals?"

Pietrangelo wiped his brow with the back of his hand. "No, but you're on the right track, doctor. Politicians."

"Both of them?" Portia asked. She assumed a married couple. Maybe he meant that the wife of a Member of Parliament would be as much a politician as her husband.

"Two old chums doing a photosafari holiday together. Woodbead, minister of Rural Affairs, and Chipping, shadow minister of Terraforming and Environment."

Portia's brow crinkled. From her age, her sex, her marital status, and the minimal amount she paid in tax less received benefits, she had too few votes to bother paying much attention to politics. But she knew the Tradition Party formed the government and Innovation provided the shadow cabinet ready to step up should the King ask them to do so.

"They're from opposite parties?" she asked. Southwark's bracelets jangled in echo of the sentiment. McAdams grunted, dissonantly.

With a glint in his eye, Pietrangelo shook his head. "Ninety percent of the rivalry you see on the news sites is staged. When the cameras are off, they raise their pints in the same pubs in New Canberra." He reached for a mug of coffee, black and steaming. "But what's important here are their portfolios. Rural affairs. Terraforming and environment." He raised a black eyebrow.

"Is the next Crown land grant up for debate?" Portia asked. A million square kilometers well to the east of Margarettown. The company sought it to extend the preserve. Farming interests wanted to turn the land over for agriculture.

A million square kilometers, far from the ongoing eruption of a volcano.

Pietrangelo nodded over a sip of coffee. "Both Woodbead and Chipping sit on the special committee tasked to draft a bill. They're old chums and they're on a fact-finding mission. Woodbead leans toward us and Chipping, the ag lobby."

"Rescuing them gives us friends in high places," said McAdams with a cynical edge in his voice.

"But I'd scramble some of my people lacking first responder training to pull out anyone, right?" Pietrangelo gave an exaggerated nod. His dark-eyed gaze drilled into Portia and the others in turn. "McAdams, Dr. Oakeshott, you're up."

"Us?" asked Portia.

Pietrangelo dismissed her doubt with a shrug. "You both have field skills. Dr. Oakeshott, you do well with people, and you can be discreet."

She looked past the COO's virtual presence as if she could see the video wall. "If the journos knew two front-bench Members of Parliament were out there, they'd be all over us."

"Like flies on cow droppings," Pietrangelo said.

Portia sat a smidgen taller. "Got it."

Southwark, the office manager, let out a pained breath. "I only have three quaddies, two Model 2000s and one 3000... and the 3000 was pulled today for routine maintenance just before we got word of the eruption."

"Then send a 2...." Pietrangelo's voice lost some firmness. "Bugger."

What was wrong with a Model 2000? A hunch came to Portia. Through her neury, she called up the specs. A quick skim confirmed her guess.

Max. combined passenger/cargo weight: 300 kg.

"A 2000 is rated to carry only four adults," Portia said, "and there are three men out there?"

"Got it in one, doctor." Pietrangelo's gaze darted to McAdams. "You'll sit this one out."

"Fair by me."

Portia's breath caught. "I'm to go alone?"

"If conditions weren't so bloody dicey, pardon my french, I'd overload the quaddy." The COO's face showed he meant the words. "The 2000's specs are overengineered, I'm sure she could carry more than a quarter ton, but tell that to the bloke off the street if two MPs suffer injury or die in an accident. Of you and McAdams, you make the most sense. If someone's hurt, I'd rather a veterinarian than a field ecologist give them first aid. And you're a good thirty kilos lighter, which might come in handy if the quaddy is flying out through turbulence."

She swallowed around a dry mouth. "I see, sir."

"Then what are you waiting for?" Pietrangelo said with a grin. "Grab your medical kit and get airborne."

The quaddy flew south-by-southeast, over farmland running from the edge of town to the preserve's perimeter. Particles blown into the air by the eruption hazed the sun behind her and the houses and barns five hundred meters below. Occasionally, grit crackled on the quaddy's front window, but nothing worse than one's rideshare might suffer sitting in traffic behind a construction site dump truck.

Distance and more haze obscured her view of the far-off volcano.

She eased back in her seat of black webbing wrapped around a nanotube alloy frame. A glance out the side window showed the last farms. Their back fences ran along the poles lining the perimeter. She had landed at a farm not far from here, perhaps the one she flew over at this very moment, in her first time ever in the field. Eighteen local years before, only about three standard. Amazing how it seemed much longer.

Farmland gave way to the deep green forest covering most of the preserve. Still hundreds of klicks from the volcano, life went on for almost all the creatures born of fossil fragments, DNA extrapolation, and Aussie pride. There grazed a herd of winners, giant four-legged herbivores of genus *Wintonotitan*. Further along, a *Kunbarrasaurus* tucked its squared-off head toward its chest, hunkering behind the bony plates covering its neck and back, while a strallo waved its stumpy arms and roared at the kunbarra through jaws of meat-rending teeth. The strallo looked skyward at the quaddy's buzzing rotors. It gave one last roar at the kunbarra, then trotted away, as if Portia's passage allowed it to give up on attacking the kunbarra while saving face.

The quaddy continued its flight. The sound of grit against the front window came more frequently. She rolled her lips together and checked the news feeds for updates on the eruption. No change—

Pang!

She jolted and looked to where the sound had come. Cracks radiated from a tiny chip of glass.

Crikey. On a much smaller scale, but exactly what had happened to the politicians' quaddy. The volcano's power had to be vast, to fling rock fragments so far from its summit.

The adrenaline jolt left a jittery feeing in her limbs. [Increase the sensitivity of your radar to above and in front,] she told the quaddy.

[Confirmed,] it replied in its bland female voice.

Two hours to go. Below, the preserve looked peaceful. Lush foliage and glimpses of dinos. Ahead, though, the haze thickened. The quaddy lurched from time to time, flinging Portia against the straps. She peered out the windows and saw nothing. A check of the quaddy's radar showed vague shadows that might be thicker clouds of particles or might be data phantoms.

For a time she shut her eyes and tightened her grips on the armrests.

She opened her eyes to see the volcano looming ahead. The angry king of the South Polar Range. Haze and clouds hid the summit. An orangey glow backlighting the clouds showed fresh lava still poured out. Amid the grays of outcropped rock and the stark whites of snow and ice visible below the cloud deck, lava streamed down the mountainside. The red-flecked orange rivers slashed across the green fuzz of forest below the tree line. The lava flows merged and broke apart at the foothills, like the delta of an ancient river on some distant world, before trickling into the flatlands of the preserve.

Huge as the volcano was, it would only loom larger. She still had twenty klicks to the rescue site. Six minutes, give or take.

She swallowed once. Her eyes darted across the streams of lava and to the hidden summit of the volcano. How much longer till the eruption stopped?

Foothills extended like long fingers away from Eighty-three's base. Hardened lava from eruptions like this one, but long ago, when the planet's skies were half carbon dioxide and lifeless were the seas. Right on time, a mossy clearing came into view on a high ridge. Lava streamed past between the ridge and its mates on both sides. The flow scoured ferns and cycads, carrying off burning trunks and leaving only thin strips of forest between the lava and the clearing.

At the clearing's north end sat a large quadrotor, with a cabin big enough to fit ten or twelve, or a smaller number in luxury. Right now, though, call it a *trirotor*. The boulder flung by the volcano lay half-embedded in the soil near the broken rotor strut. The rounded end of the rotor housing dipped nearly to the ground.

Forty meters from the luxury quaddy, the clearing held a sprawling tent, the kind that popped up with the press of a button and unfurled solar panels feeding power to an induction charger.

The quaddy descended, passing over a lava flow. Rough air shook the airframe. The rotors pulsed in an off-key chorus, automatically maximizing lift. Portia gasped and dug her fingers into her armrests. Her fingers clenched for five seconds even after the quaddy cleared the turbulence.

She watched the tent as the landing skids touched down halfway between the luxury quaddy and the tent. The plastic walls shook in the downwash of the rotors, then stilled when they rotors stopped.

Did they hear her approach? Why weren't they coming out? A look around—

She heard the shouts as she saw the them. Two men outside the luxury quaddy, waving, as behind them a third pulled down the aircraft's gullwing door.

With clumsy fingers, Portia unstrapped and pulled her veterinary kit from under her seat. Nobody looked hurt but the habit comforted her. She climbed out.

Heat hit her. Sulfur assailed her nose. Crackles and groaning snaps —a glance confirmed the lava knocked down and set fire to more trees. Ten meters of forest separated the clearing from the lava on one side, eight on the other.

As she walked toward the luxury quaddy, another sound came to her. A chitter, fast and high, gabbled out by a half-dozen voices in the trees. A loovy herd. Their long tails, banded with orange, whipped around as uneasily as a cat's. Their narrow heads darted, casting fearful glances at the humans in the clearing and at the flood of lava down the slope.

Portia's breath caught. God willing the lava flow would crest below the clearing.

"Even company employees retain their wonder at them, I see." A male voice, warm and certain of its charm.

She snapped her head around. Her neury already labeled them, projecting placards into her vision of the two men. Chipping had spoken, the one with graying sideburns and crow's feet at the corners of his eyes. Woodbead stood three centimeters taller and his lower lip tugged on his trimmed brown mustache.

"You're a sight for sore eyes, Doctor," Woodbead said. His voice sounded higher than she expected. "And ahead of schedule."

She stopped in front of them. Woodbead extended his hand and she shook his, then Chipping's. Habit, as if they met in a drawing room instead of the middle of a burning forest, and whether out of polite pommy refusal to admit to the elephant in the room or a strine urge to laugh at danger she couldn't tell and why were her thoughts running wild?

"I left Margarettown as soon as Mr. Pietrangelo apprised us of the situation. First, is anyone hurt?"

"I'm well," said Chipping. Woodbead echoed the words and the man behind them nodded. The latter took his hand away from where it smoothed his wiry black beard and tipped his digger hat to her. Ashworth his name, the tallest of the three and obviously the guide, emphasized by the standard uniform of khaki cargo shirt and pants and brown hat with brim folded up and snapped to the crown on the right side.

From the loovy herd among the trees came a low moaning. Long necks craned toward the sound. Portia recognized it instantly. An injured member of the herd.

Her heart lurched and she struggled to refocus on the two politicians. "Second, as you can see—" Portia waved her hand over her shoulder. "—the only quaddy we had available is smaller than you might have expected. It can take the three of you, but only...." She tried doing the math in her head, but between the heat and stink of the lava, the presence of two Members of Parliament, and the injured loovy, she had to use her neury. "...five kilos each of personal effects."

"Five kilos?" Chipping said. "I've collected twice that in rhyolites. The colors and textures are quite varied. Quite exquisite."

Portia's mouth worked but she couldn't come up with words. Take a cross tone with Chipping and he might harbor a grudge all the way back to Parliament House.

Behind the politicians, Ashworth rolled his eyes. When he spoke, though, his voice sounded respectful. "Sir, you can always come back after the eruption runs its course."

"Yes, but, if the lava keeps rising—"

Woodbead tipped back his head and laughed. "Then some future geologist might discover what lava does to human bones. Crikey, mate."

"Fine, fine, but give me a few minutes to pick the ones to take now." Chipping turned to Portia with a look on his face as if he hadn't just embarrassed himself. "We should have five minutes, shouldn't we?"

"The lava flow is rising slowly enough," she said. Tension switched the strings it struck inside her. "Gentlemen, pardon me." Portia shouldered her veterinary kit and went to the edge of the clearing.

Sounds of hissing steam and crackling timber filled the air. The lava stream cast orange glows through the remaining stand of cycads and ferns. The loovies' heads snapped up. Wide-set eyes, almost at a level with her own, regarded her. Their bodies squirmed and rear feet pawed at ground covered with grotesquely-bent fungi and dark green moss. Their high-pitched chitter sounded more frantic. Nostrils flared, sniffing for her across five meters.

The genetechs gave all the dinos on the preserve a deep wariness of people. Portia slowed her steps. She extended the back of her hand toward them. "Easy, you," she said softly. "I'm here to help your friend."

Their calls grew quiet. Relief filled Portia's chest. They would let her go to the wounded loovy—

A burst of chittering gave way to raucous squawks. The loovies scattered away from her, stomping through brush to her left and right within the narrow strip of forest cover between the clearing and the lava flow.

She continued into the trees. Stifling air heated her lungs. Sweat poured down her cheeks and neck. Air roared off the lava flow like from a thousand brick ovens.

Crikey, where was the wounded loovy?

Motion and sound came to her in the same instant. The loovy lifted its head far enough for a low moan to reach Portia. It lay on its side. Its tiny arms clawed weakly at the air.

Portia took a step further and winced. The loovy's tail was a charred stump, red and oozing, but its legs had suffered far worse. One leg bent at a horrid angle. Compound fractures of tibia and fibula, at a guess. The other kicked feebly, with most of its skin and half its muscle and tendon gone. What remained oozed and stank of burnt meat.

"Poor fella," she said. She took another step toward the loovy's legs, then stopped.

Part of her wanted to collapse right there and let the lava's heat dry her eyes. Nothing could be done out here for the loovy. The burn gel in her kit would cover a tiny amount of his burned skin. A degradable splint and cast might stabilize the fractures long enough to heal, but every step he took would run the risk of refracturing. Assuming the loovy could avoid the lava's scalding touch and choking heat.

Only the veterinary facility at heaquarters in Port Bounty could help him. Seven hours away. If she had room for it on the quaddy, which she didn't. A juvenile male loovy massed forty kilos if he weighed a gram.

She squeezed shut her eyes for a moment and took one breath. Steadier now, she kneeled closer to the loovy's head. He lifted his head as if trying to crawl away from her, but then it dropped back to the mossy ground. His arm pawed at her. Too weak to resist when she wrapped her grip around. Rough skin and a sparse array of stiff filaments scratched her hand.

"Easy, boy," Portia said. With one hand she pulled her veterinary kit off her shoulder. Opened the flap. Reached for a hypo containing a cocktail of anesthetic and analgesic and dialed up fifty kilos.

An overdose would be the least of the loovy's problems.

A high male voice came from the clearing. "Doctor? We're ready."

She glanced over her shoulder. Woodbead tugged at his mustache with his lower lip. "Yes?"

"We're loading the last of our items. You're ready to go?"

She felt the loovy's arm lose strength. "Almost."

"We don't have much time. The lava's flowing faster!"

Portia squeezed the loovy's arm. The purple line of a vein bulged above the loovy's skin. She injected the drug cocktail and let go of its arm. The limb drooped against its chest and a clump of electric-blue fungus.

"All done," she said. She quickly slotted the hypo back into its place in her veterinary kit, then stood and went toward the clearing. "I'm ready to go, sir."

Woodbead's small eyes ran from her to the loovy and back. "You eased its pain?"

Her gaze dropped to check her footing on the carpet of moss. "Yes."

"Good onya. A ripper thing for a sheila to do."

"Yes," Portia said. She looked behind her. The loovy's eyes had closed and his head lay slack on the fungi and moss. It breathed more slowly, despite the baking air and the crackle of another tree snapping near the base from the lava's heat and pressure. "A ripper thing."

ABOUT THE AUTHOR

I'м **Raymund Eich.** I use my Middle American upbringing as a launchpad for journeys to the ends of the Universe.

Growing up in the Midwest prepared me for my academic career, culminating with a Ph.D. in biochemistry from Rice University. It helps me help inventors prosper from their progress in medicine, biotechnology, and computer hardware.

Above all, it inspires me to write science fiction and fantasy about ordinary people facing extraordinary wonders and horrors, battling enemies both foreign and domestic, and building better lives for themselves, their families, and their societies.

My last name has one syllable and is pronounced "eye-sh." I live in Houston with my family.

Connect with me at **www.raymundeich.com** or follow the QR code below.

———

Online and brick-and-mortar bookstores around the world list millions of books, with thousands more published every day. I'm glad you discovered this one.

If you'd like to know when I release a new book, instead of leaving it to chance, join my Readers Club. I'll email you every two weeks with publishing news, book recommendations, or a short personal update.

Yes, please! I'll go to **www.raymundeich.com/mailing-list** or scan the QR code below.

No thanks. I'll take my chances next time I look for your books.

OTHER BOOKS BY THE AUTHOR

Available wherever books are sold.

Learn more about these titles at our website, **www.cv2books.com,** or follow the QR code below.

NOVELS

The Progress of Mankind

Stone Chalmers, Book 1
Complete four-book series available

Stone Chalmers. Spy. Assassin. Instrument maintaining Earth's dominion over all human worlds.

Opposing him? Hostile forces on colony worlds… and within the Earth government itself.

———

Take the Shilling

The Confederated Worlds • Book 1
Complete trilogy available

Tomas seeks an escape from his backwater planet and his widowed mother's rigid religious home.

'Taking the shilling' - enlisting as a space soldier - is only the start.

The Blank Slate

Neuroscience entrepreneur Clay Shieffer must stop a tyrannical president…
because he unwittingly gave the tyrant power over the human mind.

———

New California

After New California's founder committed suicide, two men vied to rule the
colony.

Ashwin George, supported by the colony's elite and the Chinese company
dominating half the settled galaxy.

Against him, Desmond Park, nanotechnology engineer, armed with the most
formidable weapon of all.

A single idea.

———

The Reincarnation Run

Skeptical spacejock Landry Krieger knows exactly how to smuggle the
"reborn" spiritual leader of an oppressed people past their conquerors… but
the boy's priests—and governess—shake up his orderly plans.

———

Azureseas: Cantrell's War

Ross Cantrell joined the animal control mission on the newly-discovered
planet Azureseas to earn the money to start married life together with his
girlfriend.

Then Ross discovers the truth about the planet's "animals."

SHORT NOVELS

Love and Death in the City of Bone

He had a month to solve the planet's mysteries—and Juliette's.

His cover story: return to Elard to dismantle his sect's missionary work to the planet's natives.

His true mission: investigate decades-old mysteries of love and death.

His objective: return to Earth with his discovery.

If he can.

A Mighty Fortress

Theodore and his team from the Lutheran Interstellar Terraforming Society would transform a barren, rocky world into a refuge of faith and life.

Or die trying.